Lee Maxwell was born in New Zealand and now lives on a houseboat on the outskirts of London with her two young children. *Emerald Budgies* is her first novel.

EMERALD BUDGIES

LEE MAXWELL

Grateful acknowledgement is made for permission to reprint
excerpts from the following copyrighted works:

Lyrics from 'Use Once and Destroy' (Love/Erlandson/Aus der Maur/Schemel)
© 1998 by kind permission of Universal Music Publishing Ltd.

Words by Chuck Willis taken from the song 'Sugar Sugar'
by kind permission Sony/ATV Music Publishing

Extract from *Self Help for Your Nerves* by Dr. Claire Weekes,
Angus & Robertson Publishers

First published 2000 by Diva Books
an imprint of Millivres Limited
part of the Millivres Prowler Group
116-134 Bayham Street, London NW1 0BA

A catalogue record for this book is available from the British Library

ISBN 1 873741 44 8

Printed and bound in Finland by WS Bookwell

To Greg O'Leary

Contents

1: The homesick feeling   5

2: Strange chord patterns   16

3: Tracksuit Man   20

4: Fucking hell   28

5: A tablespoon of warm sperm   43

6: Emerald budgies   50

7: What I was playing at   62

8: Flurries of minor violence   77

9: Nirvana   81

10: Hiya Ruthy   91

11: Overload   103

12: The wedding   115

13: We babies are otay now   131

14: An imbalance of carbon dioxide   133

15: All blood and bone and brown velvet   149

16: Of course I did   162

17: Oddly empty   168

18: Hermes and Aphrodite   177

19: A breath of air   188

20: The clouds, the power lines, and the moon   193

21: Forward and out   202

*Many of those who suffer from nervousness are persons
of fine sensibilities, of delicate regard for honour,
endowed with a feeling of duty and obligation. Their
nerves have tricked them, misled them.*
WR Houston

It might as well hurt.
Courtney Love

1: The homesick feeling

I saw Tracey's mother today at the supermarket. I haven't seen her for over a year and there she was gazing at the carrots like she'd never seen anything like them in her life before. *Carrots? Oh yes, I'm with you. Orange. Lovely things.*

She didn't see me – or I'm pretty sure she didn't. I was just coming in the door and I stopped dead and slapped at the space above my heart as if something monumental had just occurred to me, and then turned and ran back to the car, my heart swooping and banging around inside my chest like a poisoned old vulture. The air in the car felt too thin, like there wasn't enough to go around. There isn't... Everything stinks: the city has been marinating in its own juices for days now and an asthmatic haze hangs around the roads and buildings like the aftermath of some pointless chemistry experiment, two months into another increasingly unpredictable summer, fizzing and popping poisonously as it chugs into the bend of the 21st century.

I thought Tracey's mother might come out of the supermarket and catch me sitting there, but I didn't want to drive off because you had to pass the main entrance to get out. I wound the window down instead and tried to find the horizon to steady myself, but there was none, no freedom sea or bright sail boat, just rows and rows of empty cars and a concrete trough of shrubs. On the far side of the car park a line of warehouse buildings selling carpet and car accessories fumed in the heat.

A fat woman in white shorts smiled at me as she passed; three children trotted along beside her, poking at the shopping and picking up things. She looked normal. None of them looked like they couldn't breathe. Why wasn't *I* normal? Why couldn't that be me, bored out of my mind with my underpants showing, trundling along in the sunshine with a trolley full of fish fingers and yoghurt?

I wanted to jump out of the car and say, *Uh hi, Excuse me I can't breathe*; have one of the children hold my hand and ask mum if it would be all right if I came home with them, watched a video or something, played Batman in the bedroom – but I sat there twitching and gulping and looking anxiously out the window at them.

Anything triggers these attacks off now, anything triggers them off: it doesn't have to be frightening or surreal, or even out of the ordinary – although life is all of those things... it's the fact that the common-place can become confusing and terrifying *just like that* that makes it worse, and the fear is compounded by the knowledge that there is nothing to be afraid of, except perhaps dying or going mad.

Except perhaps dying or going mad.

I decided to try and make a run for it and managed to drive off, looking straight ahead as I passed the entrance, and then running a red light because I couldn't bear to have to stop the car again. A man shook his head at me, *stupid bitch*.

Sorry. Sorry.

What?

What?

Look, fuck off, I'm not well, all right?

Right, fucking hell, *concentrate*.

I looked in the rear-view mirror expecting to see Tracey's mother bearing down on me, but there was no sign of her. I got up to sixty on the motorway and wound the window down further to get some oxygen; the car was shaking and rattling and hot air flew around my face. I sucked at it like a little fish. A woman overtook me and looked across at me interestedly. I quickly wound the window up and turned the radio on, then flicked it off again, fumbling around for the on/off switch and nearly driving off the road.

Everything seemed larger than life, exposed: as if I were vulnerable to some bigger danger I couldn't identify. I wanted to be back home in my room, safe, with all the curtains closed, but it's too far, too big; there are too many people and just the thought of all those millions and millions and millions of people. Just the thought of them! I thought my head was going to explode. I saw the hospital coming up and braked and swerved into the car park and somehow found a space. Hospitals always gave me a sense of security – the proximity to Accident and Emergency anyway: if things took a turn for the worse I could always run in and pretend I was waiting for someone. I sat there in the car distracted with fear, wishing the sun wasn't so bright, thinking that maybe I should get out and have a little walk round. Open the door. Close it again. Open it just a... bit. Stare at my foot.

Fucking heart. Stop *beating*.

A man in a suit came rabbiting across the car park towards me carrying a bunch of roses. For one deluded moment I hoped he might stop and say *Ruth! There you are! Congratulations!* In an effort to stabilise my burgeoning madness I poked my head out of the car window and said *wow* – in a pale, bug-eyed fashion that no doubt smacked of advanced lunacy – and he glanced down at me like I was blocking his way to the stage, like he'd just picked up Best Male Performance in *Life!*, a moist acceptance speech working its way out of his back pocket, and my chair was in the way. *Thank you. Thank you everyone.*

He must have been going to maternity – I doubt whether he was expected in intensive care. (*Hello darling. That tube looks... great! I bought you these.*) Maybe the woman was someone in his office, someone he'd offered to make coffee for every day, someone he'd carefully wanked over at night under his blue striped duvet cover, and one day he reached for the mouse at the same time as she did, his long white fingers, dull hairy hand, dropping onto hers like a fly landing on the sugar, and now, *crikey*, a *baby* was lying there swaddled in a small glass cot ready to suck anything on offer; and all the while, through it all, through engagements and honeymoons, remortgaging and redecorating, it was all he could do to contain his bald and bursting heart, thanking his lucky stars to have had any part in it at all (let alone the starring role). *Thank you everyone. Thank you.*

That was what was going on for most people. Highlights.

Memorable interludes. *Happy memories.* Not this endless paranoia, this dumb hopeful thought that somewhere out there a group of people, *my friends*, were sitting round a table saying *gee Ruth's late, let's give her a few more minutes eh?*

I steeled myself for the drive home and made it somehow. After I'd been there for a few minutes I'd calmed down a bit and decided to spot some hash over the stove. Big mistake. About fifteen minutes later I was lying on the bed with the pillow over my head trying to stop myself from hyperventilating and seriously thinking about calling an ambulance. Everything sounded too loud: my breathing, the pillow scraping against my hair, and when I thought about what happened with Tracey I kind of vortexed into it and my heart started to gulp around inside my chest, hysterically, like a whale's must when it first hits the beach, when it first touches down on that firm wet sand, THUMP THUMP THUMP THUMP THUMP.

And stand by for a tetanic contraction please... *And... cue* the tetanic contraction... hold on, hold on, get those fingers to stiffen properly will you, and you're not doing the wrist bit properly, look, let me show you, like this, it's supposed to flex at the wrist like this, like a, you know, like a, *spastic* or something... OK everybody, positions *please*, right let's try that again.

No freaking way. I got up and stood in the middle of the room kneading my shoulders and burping, trying to remember where I'd put *Self Help For Your Nerves*. I finally found it in a suitcase under the bed.

> *The principle of treatment can be summarised as:*
>> *Facing.*
>> *Accepting.*
>> *Floating.*
>> *Letting time pass.*

OK I'm facing. Right, I'm facing it all, I'm accepting, I'm... *what?*, *what am I fucking doing?...* I'm *floating...* I looked further down the page to where I'd read the suggestion innumerable times before and anxiously agreed. Or *sedation*. Just the thought of sedation made me feel slightly better.

What I really need now are some tranquillisers, Valium or something, then all this will be easier to write down, it'll all seem unreal – like it wasn't me it happened to.

It's so weird that I saw her today: Tracey's mother. The supermarket's nowhere near where she lives. Maybe me just thinking about everything, squeezing it like a blind pimple, sent some form of twisted energy into the stratosphere and she latched onto it and homed in on me. That'd be right: she was big on all that. She was big full stop. Fucking massive. Eighteen stone bandaged in a lime-green T-shirt and leggings.

I forced myself to make a cup of tea, normalnormal, and came into the kitchen and saw the word processor. It's been sitting in the box on one end of the kitchen table for months, waiting. I cleared all the junk off the table and then pushed the table against the wall to make a desk, next to the power point. I found a photo of Tracey which someone (probably her) had put in a miniature silver-plated frame, and took it out of the frame and pinned it on the wall in front of me. It's one of those passport ones that you can keep changing until you're happy with the shot. It's so small that the drawing pin nearly covers her face. She's smiling. She looks like a secretary or something: it must have been one she had done for her CV. I've got other photos of her, tons of them, but I prefer this one. It has the effect of diminishing her – which gives me some sort of control over the situation.

When I was looking through the photos I found an old one of me and Ricky Forster when we were about nine. I've got bare feet and no shirt on. I've stuck that up too, next to a picture I ripped out of an interior design magazine: some American guy's place in San Juan, which sounds like it's somewhere near Mexico, and the photo is taken from the back of the room, looking out through the French windows, over the headland and out to sea. The room is full of light. You can't see the sun, but it's either just coming up or just setting, and it's casting this wonderful light across the room, onto the pale woodwork and tall wicker-backed chairs. It's the light you sometimes see in the wake of a thunderstorm, and all of a sudden you feel like you're on a film set: Vittorio Storaro's just asked for the floods to be turned on and Nastassja Kinski – a woman to die for a thousand times over for one willing kiss on those perfect lips... Nastassja is standing by, ready to drape herself all over you. And then ask if you'd like to go out after the shoot. *Oh, that is most unfortunate. Vy not?* (In my mind she is grown up, but she is not yet Americanised, her Teutonic tones whisper to me of the wild blood in her veins: of Klaus with his whoring mouth and permanent erection, satiated briefly by the sublime Biggi; of a pedigree far beyond my paltry imagination. I can't even imagine her living on the same planet as me, let alone accessible.)

Anyway, Nastassja aside, (or preferably, *inside*) I'd like to live in that house.

Dee might be able to get me some tranquillisers. Maybe they'll make me feel more normal. Have I ever been normal? I don't know. Sometimes. Sometimes I feel so normal it's weird. I sort of click into this gear where I'm not anxious at all, I'm almost *bored* by how dull everything is – when most of the time everything frightens me a little bit, especially when I see how casual and confident everyone else is. It's like they're all at the *front* of their brains looking out, and I'm somewhere way at the back of mine, staring at a great hunk of grey shit which is crossed with trip wires and empty corridors (*no point yelling lady*).

My mother used to call me – among other things, this was one of her more favourable descriptions – *fickle*: if she was sitting at the kitchen table with Mrs Forster who used to come over and go on about her husband (*thanks for that* she'd say as she was leaving), my mother would say, right in front of me, *Of course, Ruth here's very fickle,* and then she'd stare at me like I was an egg that she'd dropped on the concrete and say, *God knows who she got it from.*

(This is from a woman who would send my father humphing back to the kitchen with her cup of tea because it was too cold or too weak or had too much sugar or tasted like *cat's piss*. *Don't bother Alan*, she'd sigh, hoisting herself out of her chair, the TV guide falling to the floor, *I'll do it myself*.)

I remember when I was a kid I would lie in bed at night too scared to move, imagining that I had this huge huge head and a tiny distorted doll's body, and the night outside would stretch into infinity and I was incapable of stopping myself being sucked into it and my head would just get bigger and bigger until it *was* the universe and I was nothing. And then sometimes during the day I'd get what I used to call the homesick feeling. When I think about it it's always stifling hot: it's the middle of summer and I'm in my bedroom sitting on the edge of my bed plucking at the orange candlewick bedspread and I'm looking up at a piece of hard blue sky through my bedroom window which is covered in fly shit, and I'm feeling homesick – but I know I can't be because... *I am already at home.*

Tranquillisers and heroin are about the only things that make me feel normal these days, the way I imagine most people must feel all of the time. (I don't take heroin that often. I'm not sure why; sometimes I think I'd be better off if I just stayed there – stopped kidding myself that there was anything worth coming home for.)

Drugs. Christ. I can hear the protest now. You're not still taking *drugs* are you? Have you tried colonic irrigation dear? A litre and a half of water every day? Clary sage oil in a burner's supposed to be very good too. (And out there every weekend entire ocean liners of drugs are still being sucked up for fun, for no reason, because we want to.)

I'd had some Valium the night I first met Tracey. James had been plying me with vodka for most of the night before presenting me with 20mg of Valium as an inducement for going to the club with him because he didn't want to go by himself.

Gay clubs were usually lonely places for me, populated as they were with gay men and small groups of self-contained, out-for-the-evening lesbians: nobody so much as looked at me most of the time – I could have been invisible – except for the odd dominatrix type, some strange dwarf in riding breeches who saw something hopeful in me. I obviously reeked of BISEXUAL as opposed to LESBIAN, which always made me feel like an imposter, but I'd had just enough vodka to forget that for the moment, and I wanted the Valium, so I agreed.

I saw Tracey the minute we walked in. She was gorgeous: tall with shoulder-length blonde hair, expensively cut so that it looked careless, and she had her arms wrapped around a tiny woman in a red dress who was so drunk she could hardly stand up.

I remember I couldn't stop looking at her: I wanted to take her home and kiss her, kiss her till her lipstick was smeared all over my face, tell her that I loved her, would always love her, and then take her to bed with me and live happily ever after. And I wanted to mainly because I wanted to see if I *could*.

I'd like to say it had a more glorious beginning than that, but the truth is it didn't. I can still see myself now spiralling lazily around the dance floor grinning at James and the other gayboys as they wound themselves into the usual weekend drug frenzy (the occasional shriek indicating an epiphany of sorts) and glancing at her periodically to see if she was looking. Which she was.

When she went to the toilets I trailed her like a hyena and stood two behind her in the queue. I didn't want to go to the toilet myself so once I got inside I stood behind the door imagining the time it would have taken to have undone my trousers etc., and listening to see if I could hear her come out. I timed it perfectly: she was washing her hands when I opened the door and she smiled at me in the mirror which took me by surprise... one doesn't expect the wildebeest to present themselves quite so readily. I smiled back and followed her through the crowd. Her girlfriend grabbed her arm and they laughed about something, and even though she didn't look up to see if I was watching, I knew she knew I was, because she went into show-mode after that, became principal boy in the panto, cavalierly swinging the smaller girl onto her knee where she perched like a ventriloquist's dummy, smiling and waggling her little legs about.

A praying mantis couldn't have done a better job. I stood where she could see me and just stared at her: as if I could hypnotise her into flinging the little dolly off her knee and coming and asking me for my phone number.

The gayboys thought it was a great game, appearing at my side every few minutes and egging me on with a series of just fucking do its, ask her to dance, now, while her girlfriend's at the bar, go on, *go girl*, go get her.

So of course I did. *Why wouldn't I have?* I went up to her and said would she like a dance, and next thing we were jerking around the dance floor yelling over the music.

"I'm Ruth!"

"Hi, I'm Tracey!"

"Hi Tracey! What do you do?"

"Nothing!" She did a little twisty hand movement to the music, "I was doing a media studies course but I didn't like it!"

"Why's that?"

"Boring!"

She looked at me and grinned. I grinned back.

"I'm gay!"

I didn't think I'd heard her properly.

"You're *what?*"

"Gay!" she said and spun around, singing along to the music.

I would have thought it was perfectly obvious that she was gay, and in a more sober frame of mind been slightly puzzled by this bizarre admission, but that night all I thought was Fucking Great. Gorgeous. Talented. Gay.

Gay gay gay.

Yip fucking ee. Yabba dabba doo. Ya fucking hoo, and other patheticisms I have since come to Bitterly Regret: one cliché – *myself* – deserving another.

Maybe I just got stuck in a time warp and stayed fourteen years old. Or perhaps I really am a man, like she said once. *Come on Ruth, admit it.*

We'd only been dancing for about a minute when her girlfriend came back from the bar. She stood on tiptoe and yelled something into Tracey's ear before ploughing back to their table and falling into a chair, where she sat glaring at us.

"Is that your girlfriend?" I yelled.

Tracey looked uneasy and yelled back that she'd better go, but did I have a phone number where she could call me at some stage? Yo burger. It took me half an hour to find a pen: I had to traipse around the club asking people who kept staring at me like I'd just asked them to fuck me up the arse with a Coke bottle, *No, no it has to be Coke*, and then it took another hour before I could corner Tracey by herself at the bar, where I did an intense staring *I look forward to it* number on her before tripping off dramatically into the night, mission complete, not bothering with a cab, not caring about all the rapings and stabbings and robbings that might befall me, feeling just like Holly Golightly – although this laissez-faire attitude was more than likely a result of the Valium – and finally arriving home at about four in the morning.

I felt like I did when I was a kid and got second in the breaststroke championships even though I couldn't dive. At the start of the race I had to go over and whisper to the starter if it was all right if I got into the pool. He told me to speak up and made me repeat myself before directing me to the edge of the pool: all eyes on me now as I slid down the side of that cold cliff, grazing my leg, the other girls positioning themselves expertly on the starter blocks waiting for the gun to propel them gracefully into the air while I pushed off from the end. My face was so hot it could have made the water boil. I remember I nearly made myself sick as I passed them all but one on the last length. I got a certificate and a yellow ribbon which went some way towards making up for the humiliation of my belly flops into the local pool at the weekends, my father holding a hoop for me to dive through again and again, my skin red and stinging from the repeated slaps against the water, the hoop flattening out and trapping me on the surface as I tried to remember to keep my head tucked beneath me. *Keep your chin down*, he'd yell at me, *For God's sake girl.*

She rang me the following Tuesday at work. I was a PA for LIZ BAILEY PUBLIC RELATIONS – Liz did everything in capitals – but she was on holiday so there wasn't much happening. I was sitting at my desk cleaning my fingernails with a paperclip and thinking about going home when the phone rang.

"Hi, is that Ruth? It's Tracey. We met at the club."

To do or not to do. The Friday night euphoria had worn off by then, and it all seemed like it was a bit of a dream. I couldn't remember exactly what she looked like either. And there was bound to be a design fault: there always was. Some horror to be unearthed: a rogue penis, or raped at birth by the midwife or something. Common sense versus drug-addled lechery. (Plus Maxine down on reception seemed to be warming to my *Isn't everybody bisexual?* conversations.)

"I met you at the club. Don't you remember?"

I thought about her with her arms wrapped around the small woman in the red dress.

"Oh hi, sorry," I said, "I was just thinking about something else – did you get home all right?"

"Yeah, I'm still feeling shagged though," she said and giggled at the double entendre of it all. "Sorry, I'm nervous."

"That's OK, so am I."

Liar, liar.

Pants on fire.

2: Strange chord patterns

Dee's not on the phone but she's usually at home: she doesn't do much except trail back and forth from the chemist to get her methadone. She only comes round here when she's got no money. She tells people she's a landscape gardener, and keeps a few tools in the back of her van in case any jobs come up. I met her at the library of all places. She was getting told off by the librarian for kneeling in front of a shelf reading, instead of using a chair. Dee's written a book, a novel, about ten years ago but couldn't get it published. She showed me all the rejection slips one day, but not the book. She won't even tell me what it's about, but judging from the fading letters from publishers it's some sort of personal odyssey: *"... But does one not weary of it after a while?... I felt it was the author speaking, that there wasn't a clear enough sense of the narrator as a character... deeply self-reflexive..."*

When I got home I looked up self-reflexive in the dictionary hoping that the Geraldine who'd written it had got the word wrong – that it was supposed to be reflective or something – but it meant "introspective: directed back upon itself or its own operations". It made me want to read Dee's book all the more, but she won't let me. It's shit, she says.

I feel like crying when she says that, but then that's not unusual.

The week I met Dee she conned me into letting her prune the big pine tree in the back garden. I left her with her dog, Mack, roaring around pooing everywhere, and went into town. By the time I got back she'd practically chopped the entire tree down, it was basically a trunk with a few severed branches left near the top, and she was drinking peach schnapps, the chainsaw futtering blue smoke on the lawn beside her. Everything looked raw and wounded, and the flower beds were pressed flat and steaming with dog shit. Mack was chewing a piece of grass and surveying his handiwork while Dee knocked back the last of the schnapps. In the middle of the lawn she'd built a drunken bonfire of branches, as tall as she was. And the smell! It was every Christmas and all summers rolled into one. I couldn't believe the carnage. Fortunately, she had her back to me and didn't see me – Mack did, but he ignored me – so I locked myself in the bathroom until they left half an hour later, after she'd ransacked the kitchen looking for more alcohol. She doesn't say goodbye most of the time anyway, she just drives off, tyres squealing, stereo full blast. The neighbours stare at me for days after she's been around. Not that I blame them. Dee looks like a drag queen gone to pack, and she's usually drunk.

She likes gin, so I took her a bottle of that. I didn't really want to go out again: I'd only just recovered from the supermarket episode, but the thought of getting some Valium spurred me on.

The traffic was passing in fits and starts, braking and accelerating over the hump directly in front of the house, pouring more shit into the air. It took me over an hour to get to her place... watch *out*... get out of my fucking way you fuck. I was shaking by the time I pulled up in front of her flat. She was sitting on the front step in the sun with the door open, smoking. I waved and she watched me get out of the car, looking me up and down as I walked in the gate towards her: a drug-addicted cattle dealer faced with a mutated cow. *Come on, what'll ya give me for it? Eh? Eh?*

"How the fuck are ya?" she asked, taking a drag on her cigarette and flicking ash into a terracotta pot that had some ants and a dry stick in it.

"OK." I passed her the gin and sat on the step beside her. She opened the bottle and had a mouthful.

"Want some?"

"No thanks. You haven't got any Valium or anything have you?"

"Na," she said, picking her toenails, not looking at me.

"Sorry."

This was like a ritual to Dee. She always said no and then left me waiting for hours, days, while she made endless cups of coffee, or watched TV, or fucked around in the bathroom, and then she'd say to wait in the van, we were going to see Willy or Mickey or whoever, and I knew we were going to score whatever it was I'd asked her for. It all had some significance that I didn't understand.

Today she took off in the van and didn't come back for nearly two hours, leaving me sitting in the lounge drinking gin and looking through her books. Every room, including the toilet, is full of books. Carlos Castaneda; *The Whole Earth Catalogue*; *Batik Made Easy*. When you open them you sometimes catch a faint hint of patchouli oil, which makes me think of velvet patchwork quilts in converted buses, long velvet dresses: Dee when she was young (was there ever such a thing?).

When she finally got back she subjected me to a terrifying trip across town with Mack being thrown around in the back alternatively yelping and threatening to rip people's throats out. Mack's been in three car accidents so far – the last one on the motorway when he got hurled out of the passenger window – so now, whenever he skids across the back seat, a look of comic horror on his doggy face, Dee tries to make it up to him by turning around in her seat and slurring, *Nearly there Macky, nearly there boy*, while I'm in the front clawing at my seat belt screaming *Dee! Car! Car! Car!* or *Red Light! Red Light! Red Light!*

The gin helped. It gave me a sense of bravado anyway. (Fifteen years old and heading for the beach, a bag of pot and a sleeping bag in the back, up for anything.)

I was drunk by the time we got to where we were going which was somebody called Ray's house who apparently had some Valium. I hurt my ankle as I got out of the van and Mack nearly knocked me over as he lunged towards a cat on the other side of the road, just missing a car.

"Mack! You fuck!" Dee screamed at him and he stopped for a second and looked back at her before plunging down the side of the house.

"Fucking dog." She left him there and we swaggered into Ray's swigging on the gin.

Ray turned out to be a sweet, balding man dressed in a white shirt and grey trousers. He was in his late twenties, or maybe thirties: I couldn't tell. He had a Casio keyboard set up in the lounge. He shuffled around and made us a cup of coffee and we poured gin into it which tasted disgusting but I was past caring. They had some heroin and I sat there looking at nothing in particular, toying with the idea of having some too. As Dee stuck the needle into Ray's arm he closed his eyes and breathed *All right… OK*, like he was telling himself he was. *It's going to be all right…* Fuck. Strange how things creep up on you all the time. Like Tracey's fucking mother. I decided to have some, and had my turn. We sat there for several hours, not saying much, just drinking coffee and wandering into the toilet occasionally to throw up. I talked to Ray about his keyboard. He plays in a jazz band on the weekends. He is so softly spoken that I had to lean forward across the table to hear him. Mack arrived at the door and galloped in, knocking over Ray's keyboard before heading out the back and running around in circles on the tiny patch of lawn, growling and snapping at his tail. Ray picked up his keyboard and played strange chord patterns for us; I gave him the money for the Valium and left them watching TV while I caught a cab back to Dee's and drove (smoothly, nervelessly) home.

I'm back now. I've started. I've reported for duty. I keep looking at the needle mark in the crook of my arm like a child with a secret might, and knowing I've got some Valium (I've had one already) makes me feel reasonably secure, as though I can sit here by myself, if not *forever*, then at least for the time needed to tell this story.

3: Tracksuit Man

Tracey and I arranged to meet in a bar on Friday night after work. She was at the back of my mind all week: like something in the back of the fridge which has to be consumed before the cream goes off. I got there ten minutes late (in the hope of being late) but she wasn't there. The place was packed but I got a glass of red wine and managed to get a seat by the window. A few minutes later I saw her trotting down the footpath towards the bar. She had a peculiar running style, like a mesmerised tribesman settling in for a twenty-mile stint, spear akimbo. I watched her come in the door and then continued to stare fixedly out the window as though I hadn't seen her. She arrived with the waiter in tow, flushed.

"Hi!" she said exuberantly. "Sorry I'm late."

"Hello," I said, suddenly feeling embarrassed.

I tried to take in as much as I could while she was struggling out of her jacket. She was like a puppy. All paws and eyes. Not particularly graceful but beautiful in that blonde way men seem to like. She was wearing a fifties-style black cocktail dress with a long-sleeved black lycra vest beneath it, and black tights. The glamorous student. I couldn't see her shoes. Yellow nail polish, and three or four colourful bracelets. And tall. At least four inches taller than me. She'd been tall in the nightclub but I didn't remember her being *that* tall. I leaned around the table to look at her shoes.

"I like your shoes," I said.

"Thanks."

She smiled and handed the waiter her jacket.

"Would you like a drink?" he asked sharply.

"Sorry," she smiled at him, "hi."

"Hi," he said, feigning boredom.

"Um, yes please." She looked at my glass. "Red wine please."

He sauntered off, clicking his pen.

"Hi," I said, "sorry. I just want to go to the toilet. Do you mind?"

"No." She sat down, still smiling. Her entrance hadn't gone unnoticed: a suave stockbroker type at the next table was leaning back in his chair, lighting a cigarette while her surveyed her. I rushed off to the toilets to have a line. She was gorgeous – I'd got that right – but completely flat-chested. Why didn't I ever *look*?

I didn't want to appear too keen so I stopped at the bar on the way back to have a conversation with a woman about how great it was they had bowls of corn chips on the tables. She was as thrilled as I was by the end of it. When I finally got back to the table Tracey was talking to the waiter, who was now half-sitting in my seat.

"Well, here we are," I said, after he'd gone.

"Here we are."

"I think he's in love." He was now watching her intently from the bar.

"Is he?" She screwed up her nose. "I don't know. Cheers."

"Cheers."

We each had a sip of our drink and looked around. Our eyes caught on the return journey.

Hers were blue. Her eyelashes had gunky blue mascara on them.

"What?" she said and laughed.

"Nothing. I was just looking at your eyes."

This didn't faze her in the slightest. "You were in the toilet a long time," she said, holding the glass coyly to her mouth.

"Was I?"

"What were you doing?"

"Nothing." *Everything* my smile said. "Do you want some?" I laughed.

"Yeah? What is it?"

"Nothing. Just some cocaine."

I didn't normally call it cocaine but it sounded more impressive than coke. I never knew what to call heroin until I settled for just plain heroin: smack sounded stupid, so did scag, and horse was entirely out of the question. Not that I'd ever met anyone who called it horse.

"Did you have it in the toilet?"

No I had it on the table here in front of you.

"Sorry. I wasn't sure if you wanted any."

She nodded, uncertain as to what to say next. (It was one of her more endearing traits, this uncertainty, although I became increasingly cynical about it as I got to know her because she was always so aware of what she was saying, and the effect she was having, that I couldn't help but think she somehow calculated this hesitancy because it made her look less greedy than she actually was.)

(Or maybe that just describes *me*.)

I didn't really want to give her the coke because I didn't have much left, but I had some trips in my bag, real ones, which I'd been carrying around for months, too scared to touch.

The office where I worked with Liz was above a radio station called HarmonyFM and Liz was friends with one of the DJs, Danny Wayne. *Good afternoon, I'm Danny Wayne, here with you right through this afternoon, and... how ya doin'?* He had a big round head and a paddock of black hair that accentuated the size of it, as if his occupation demanded a visible expression of his egotism. Liz was shouting him lunch one day, notching up a few favours, and while he was waiting for her to get off the phone he strutted around in his pot-bellied T-shirt using my rubbish bin as an ashtray and reading everything on my desk. Before he left he slipped me the trips and winked.

"I've got some acid," I said now, feeling foolish saying it. "Would you like half a trip?"

"Are you having one?" she flirted.

"Yeah, might as well."

"All right."

We smiled at each other again and I found the acid and popped half on my tongue, then indicated that she should open her mouth for the other half. My finger touched her tongue as I placed the acid on it and a promising look passed between us.

After a couple more glasses of wine her breasts were beginning to look decidedly attractive. She was by far the most gorgeous looking woman in the bar.

And I was with her.

Cheap thrill.

Just the kind I liked. Like wanking in a public place or something, in the office toilets and you've got your hand down your pants while outside the door the receptionist puts her lipstick on in the toilet mirror: close enough for you to hear the pop of the lipstick tube opening and then the beating silence as it's applied. And maybe, *just maybe*, if you can hear her, she can hear you: she can hear the quiet scraping of masturbation from behind the toilet door and wonder what – who? – it is. *Surely* not?

Tracey and I sat there drinking – or knocking them back would be a more accurate description of the frenzied ordering and reordering that was going on – and at some stage the acid kicked in and we were raving at each other about TV and trips and girls, and the effect we were having was like the best drug in the whole fucking world. I was running my foot up and down her leg, and she was stroking my hand, and we were centre stage. Everyone else in the bar became a voyeur whether they liked it or not: the men imagining both of us fucking, the women wondering what it would be like to sleep with a woman, the gayboys lapping it all up, and two round-shouldered lesbians in the corner ignoring us because we weren't real lesbians – i.e. two ugly fucks like they were. When I said that, Tracey looked shocked and said, *I can't believe you just said that!* then quickly checked her own reflection in the window, shaking her head about like a pony.

Tracey liked to champion anything uglier than herself, that's if they were human. (Except for her mother, I later found out.) In the animal department she didn't bother with such artifice: she cut to the quick and went for maximum impact. Adorable kittens, thoroughbred horses or splendid looking dogs were all patted or pointed out, and she was always the first to do this, so that whatever anybody said after that, that they too thought the kitten was lovely, or the horse amazing, just ended up sounding like a confirmation of her own good taste. It was a very irritating habit which had the effect of shutting me up, but I don't think it ever occurred to her that this was the reason I'd gone cold, or wandered away. I think she just thought I didn't like animals *(oh but I did, Tracey)*, or I was just generally bad tempered. Even though she was smart, she wasn't smart enough to see this in herself, which was one of the reasons I never fell in love with her.

But I wanted to fuck her.

In the beginning.

(Well, at least once, anyway.)

We were parked under a street light in the car park around the corner from the bar. We'd walked back to the car arm in arm under the guise of keeping warm. I ran the engine and turned the heater on and we talked for a while, and then we kissed – I thought she would smell of jonquils, green grass, honeysuckle, but she smelt slightly off. Like old milk. *I'm halfway down the bus. I'm sitting in the dark next to a farm hand who's going home to see his parents. I can't really see what he looks like but he's got long hair. I'm fourteen. I kiss him. I am so anonymous I can do anything. A jack-in-the-box forces itself into my hand as I proudly undo his zip. Pubic hair. And there's something else. A horrible smell. What is that? I try breathing through my mouth but I can't, it's got a fence post in it. I'm gagging on whatever that is coming out of him. I have to swallow it – there's nowhere else for it to go. I'm shocked but I'm acting casual. I sit up and stare out the front window. Car headlights run over my face. My mouth is alive with that liquid. There's something strange about that liquid.* I stroked her face and throat and moved my hand down to her breasts, searching for any protuberance which might indicate a nipple. I found one and squeezed it.

"*Don't.* Don't do that."

"What?"

"That hurts."

"Sorry," I pulled her face around and kissed her, pushing my tongue into her mouth. "You like it though, don't you?"

"No."

"Yes you do," I said, pinching her nipple harder. "You love it."

I tugged at her dress and together we pushed her clothes up under her armpits.

Her tits were horrible: tiny, oblique cones with insipid pink nipples that looked like they'd been sucked by a calf. They had no definition, like plasticine. I pulled at them and she moaned and arched her back, offering them to me, and opening her legs. I reached into her tights to pull lightly at her pubic hair, my middle finger bending down awkwardly into the warm slit.

A group of people came into the car park, walking towards us to their car. I sucked the nipple closest to me, and rolled the other one between my fingers. She tried to push my head away.

"There's someone coming."

"Good." I held her nipple between my teeth and listened while the polite laughter and footsteps got closer. Tracey stopped struggling and rested her head on the headrest, moaning and stroking my hair. I sucked at her nipple and she held my head tightly and pushed her cunt up hard against my elbow as everything went insanely quiet, and car doors opened and closed. An engine started and I looked up to see four middle-aged faces all desperately looking forward except for the driver – a man of about fifty who was staring at us like he was either going to throw up or come – and I looked right at him and tilted my head back so he could get a better view and lapped at Tracey's tit like a cat in the orange neon light.

All very rock 'n' roll.

But does one not weary of it after a while?

One does, yes. One does.

***

She hadn't told her girlfriend where she was going so I dropped her a few doors away and watched her walk inside. The outside light was on and she gave me a little wave. I was glad when the door closed.

I drove home pretending I was a rally driver, head dipped, easing it into third, pre-empting the traffic lights. The wind had picked up and plastic bags and empty crisp packets sailed around the street lights. I sat in the car in front of my flat listening to the wind in the trees. A small round shape bumbled down the footpath towards me and stopped beside the car. A hedgehog. I got out and touched it with my boot. It curled up, waiting for me to go. There was a plastic bag fluttering along the footpath so I ran after it and jogged back, carefully positioning it over the hedgehog and then scooping it up into it. It flipped neatly into the bag and I tied the handles into a tight knot around it. The tips of its spikes came through the plastic. I wedged the bag into the space between the back tyre and the road, got into the car, and slowly backed up. I felt the bag crunch under the back wheel, and imagined the spikes puncturing the tyre. My heart was whirring away like an electric pump, but I couldn't stop: I went forward and back, forward and back, until it must have been completely flattened, and then not wanting to look, locked the car doors and went inside.

James was in the lounge watching a porn video with some oily little boy of about fourteen who looked like he spent most of his life in a doorway. The whole room stunk. James looked at me and giggled.

"Hi-eeee," he said. "This is my friend Darren."

Darren looked sullenly in my direction.

"Tracey rang for you," James said.

"What, *now?*"

Two men in a sauna were grunting and groaning on screen, one of them about to stick an enormous penis into the other's upturned arse. *Oh yeah. Ih. Mm. Come on baby.* The three of us stared heavily at the TV and I knew I was in for another night of drum samples punching against my bedroom wall, and the smell of amyl nitrate seeping under my door (and, quite possibly by the look of him, Darren threatening to commit suicide at first light, shit and semen dribbling down his leg as he bolted for the door).

"What did she want?"

"What's that, love?" James said, rubbing the boy's knee through his filthy trousers.

"Tracey."

"What?" he said, smiling lewdly at him.

"Forget it. Goodnight."

I went to my room and ten minutes later James's bedroom door slammed shut and his CD player came on. I thought about the hedgehog and whether I'd have to scrape it off the wheel or not. What if I had a flat tyre? I stood in front of the mirror and looked at my face. What a mess. The pores on my cheeks looked enormous, and there were blackheads all over my nose. I looked like a rat on acid.

There didn't seem much point in trying to get to sleep so I had the last of the coke and went out the back door to find a stick. The breeze had picked up and the trees were all waving madly to the wind as it sprinted south. I stood at the door for a moment grinding my teeth and wondering what Tracey wanted at three in the morning. Pity about her tits. Still, she was definitely an easy fuck. No doubt about that. I found a branch and went around the side of the house to the street. There was a man crouched beside my car. He was tall and thin with white wispy hair tucked behind his ears and he was wearing a dirty grey tracksuit. He had the plastic bag in his hand, and blood was dripping out of it, onto his hand and onto the road. "It's all right," he was saying, *speaking softly to the bag*. "It's going to be OK..."

Then he looked up and saw me.

Like he'd known me all my life.

4: Fucking hell

"I think you imagined it," Maxine said, ripping open a paper bag and taking out a custard square, or something that resembled a custard square: the family at the bakery hadn't quite perfected the colour – this one was a shimmering sulphuric yellow stuck to a plank of the Vietnamese equivalent of shortcrust pastry. She took a bite and went back to the magazine she'd been reading. I was sitting beside her at reception looking at her makeup while we talked. I'd arrived at work early: a few sales reps hopped about the place but the phones were relatively quiet.

Maxine's makeup was perfect. Even around her nose. Just the right consistency. Her red lipstick was shiny and thick and she'd outlined her lips with black lip liner. I touched my own cracking lips with my tongue.

"What about Ultra – ?" She looked at the page, puzzled. "Ultra Rapid Opiate Detoxification?"

Maybe I should buy some mascara like that.

"No?" she said and raised her eyebrows at me before quickly flicking through the rest of the magazine.

Maxine wanted to be in a band and her current preoccupation was trying to think up a name for it. Rick, her boyfriend, was teaching her how to play guitar when he wasn't *gigging*. She'd dragged me along to two of his *gigs* and the same people had been there both times. Her sister. His parents came to one. He was appalling. Big thirty-second guitar solos with his ponytail tied up with one of her hair ties.

This brush with glory had been the petrol on the fire of Maxine's own ambition which was sitting cross-legged with a cigarette lighter somewhere in the hard-rock arena. Her main drawback was that she didn't know how you actually wrote a song – she went for the nebulous *you'll have to wait and see* line – but dressed for the part anyway, a sort of gothic office-girl look, and dreamt of being on stage (oh yeah) behind a shiny, low-slung guitar with thousands of hysterical boys undulating in slow motion beneath her.

Or I presumed she did. I doubt whether she was dreaming about me, down there on reception. Not that I would have minded. She was nice. I liked the combination of tailored trousers and lizard tattoo, and invested a fair amount of energy into flirting with her. Whenever I got her on the phone I'd lower my voice a couple of octaves and say *And what are you doing?* She'd say *Nothing,* or *What do you think I'm doing?* or *Come down and see me for coffee.* It was all bullshit but I lived in hope. Of what I don't know. The reality would be a drunken fumble which she'd hate, and then she'd tell Rick who'd want to sleep with us both, which wasn't going to happen, and that would set off a nice patch of rot in some dank corner of their relationship. Yay.

Maxine was the receptionist for HarmonyFM: a rabbit warren of teal-blue nylon carpeting, and airless production studios with doors so heavy you had to put your coffee down before you could open them (and then they'd suck shut behind you, banging you in the back, making you spill your coffee anyway). The station had recently been sold to some radio conglomerate and they'd shipped in a few hired guns to *sort the place out.* A new Programme Director had started, Dan, who spent his days roaming around his duck-blue kingdom, off to the studio to find out *What the fuck was going on,* or out for a bit of business. The business being a minimum of two bottles of wine – for Dan was your real boozer *mate,* a closet pants wetter and footpath vomiter – over maximum point scoring, with a veiled mention of whatever he was doing there tagged on the end. The real business he did on the phone: Dan didn't appear too keen on direct eye contact. Dan liked memos. A memo had been sent round telling staff that the station's call sign was *not* 81, OR 81FM, but *Easy Listening HarmonyFM.* NOTHING ELSE WOULD DO. Maxine had to answer the phones with: *Good (morning/afternoon). Pause. Welcome to Easy Listening HarmonyFM. Pause. (Insert your name here) speaking. How can I help you?*

There was only one copywriter on station, a woman called Sue who chain-smoked and was always in a bad mood, and an entire wing of sales reps who had one thing in common: the pursuit of money (but, as befitted the ailing fortunes of the radio station, they were always several steps behind it, cursing and clutching at their sides, only catching up with it long enough to pull at the waistband of its shorts before it eased ahead again). Sales was *under review* but *the guys* kept up a good front anyway, bristling about in their clean underwear, just about to get out of the car park lift, or into the car park lift, briefcases full of high hopes and pristine contract pads.

Liz and I were upstairs next to Andrew and Mace who did computer graphics and were permanently stoned: they were like two little moles blinking in the light, trying to look vaguely businesslike in their bobbled jumpers.

Maxine was definitely a star turn down on reception. John Titus, the accountant, was always stopping in front of her desk to do his Pete Townshend guitar-hero pose, arm whirling around, suit trousers riding up over his socks, thrilled with himself. Tightarse fancied her, but then so did most of the males in the building (and me of course), and in lieu of something really exciting happening to her, Maxine jollied everyone along, a willing terminal for any spare office desire. *Hey, looking good Max*, the DJs in their bomber jackets left over from their Top 40 years would nod at her as they swung by, clutching CDs and fan mail, eyes flicking chestwards, *very nice*. The women would just comment on bra size and difficulty running.

The DJs were OK: mostly they were just trying to get stuff for free – new cars or pizza vouchers or helicopter rides. Any fucking thing.

I liked them actually – they reminded me of third-rate circus performers, slapping on their cheap greasepaint and forgetting where they'd put their caravan keys – but I hated working for Liz. Maxine was about the only thing keeping me there and she was looking for a new job. I kept saying she had to take me with her. She didn't seem averse to the idea.

I'd told her about the trip and the man kneeling beside my car in the middle of the night, but I hadn't told her about the hedgehog bit.

"Did you say anything to him?" she said, writing *It* in red felt tip on a piece of A4 paper and then holding the paper up.

"Yeah, I asked him in for coffee," I said, "and then we had sex."

"Really?" she said, and smiled obligingly, writing *It It It* in huge letters on the paper. The phone rang and she rolled her eyes. It was somebody wanting to know what song was on before the seven o'clock news. Maxine tried to fob them off with a *Can you ring back later?* which didn't look like succeeding so I gave her a wave and went upstairs. I made a cup of coffee and sat in Liz's chair drinking it. A blast of obscure heavy metal came mincing up through the floor: the breakfast DJ cutting loose, winding the volume up on his middle age, flailing his arms around in a drum frenzy. Poor bastard. The phones would be going berserk.

I couldn't stop thinking about Friday night. After I'd seen the psycho by my car I'd run down the side of the house and in through the back door, slamming and locking it behind me. I sat in the middle of my bed with my crocheted blanket pulled tight around my shoulders, freaking out. What a fucking *weird guy*. Maybe the acid was stronger than I'd thought. I sat there listening to the wind and straining to hear any sounds of forced entry (beside James's that was) when it suddenly occurred to me that I wouldn't have been able to hear *anything* he'd said, not as clearly as I had, because it was gale force outside – he would had to have been *yelling* for me to have heard him at all.

Fucking hell.

I spent the next few hours getting in and out of my pyjamas and opening and closing drawers and looking at myself in the dressing table mirror. The wind finally dropped around five and I ventured into the kitchen to make a cup of tea. It was all quiet on the homo front – just the fetid smell of carnality hanging listlessly around the hallway. The kitchen was a disgusting mess as usual. A flannel was sitting on one end of the bread board, next to hundreds of dirty coffee cups, and glasses with soggy lemon and cigarette butts floating in them, used teabags, the entire cutlery drawer, and some leftover Chinese takeaways.

I lay crumbled under my blanket on the couch drinking tea and watching TV and waiting for James to surface. I felt really strange. Shaky and hot, then cold, then disgusted with myself and everything I stood for. (*Did I stand for anything?*) The shower finally came on at about eleven and James emerged with a skimpy towel flopping round his waist and his ears full of shaving cream. His nose was crimson and there was a poisonous blue amyl tinge around his nostrils.

"James," I said, desperate for him to have a look outside, "I think we had a prowler."

"You're *joking*." His hand rushed to his mouth. "*Darren,*" he squealed, "we've had a prowler!"

"That's nothing to what I've just given him, love," he added humourlessly before heading for the kitchen.

I went after him. He rummaged around under the sink and found a plastic mixing bowl and got himself muesli and milk and then stood there chewing it, looking at me vacantly.

"Cup a tea?" he said.

"Will you look outside for me?"

He ignored me and walked out of the kitchen with his muesli. I made another pot of tea and took it into the lounge. The CD player was on again. I banged on his bedroom door and yelled *Your tea's here!* and he came into the lounge a few minutes later looking pleased with himself, still in his towel.

"Don't you ever think about anything else?"

"What else is there to think about?" he said, sitting down girlishly on the couch and pulling my blanket around his legs.

"I don't know. *Anything*. All you think about is coming."

"So? What do you think about? Cunt?"

"Don't be so disgusting."

"What's disgusting about that? You seem to like it."

He looked like a puffball. If I pushed my finger into his face, green stuff would explode everywhere.

"Can I have my blanket back please?"

There was a mean silence which rearranged itself after a few seconds.

"Have I got a sex addiction then?" he said, tucking his knees artfully under his chin.

"I think so."

"Do you?"

"Yes I do."

"Oh." He drew it out, like a child might. "Have I got a problem then?"

This was a typical James ploy, paradoxically designed to take the heat off himself. We'd had this conversation a hundred times before. I always fell for it and would helpfully list all the hobbies he might take up and all the directions his life might take if he employed half the energy he used on trying to have sex. Then I'd touch on exploitation, and age difference, and AIDS, and he would sit there looking worried, and nodding and agreeing, until I was exhausted.

As usual this time when I'd finished my spiel he looked suitably contrite and then inspired and then promptly launched into a diatribe about how he'd nearly had Miro last night but Miro had gone off with Matthew because Matthew had given him some acid but he wasn't worried because his real friends wouldn't do that to him and anyway he didn't care because he'd got Darren. (He conveniently omitted to say where he'd got Darren *from*.) Ignoring the look on my face he then went into graphic detail about Darren's arsehole and how he'd sucked it out and then wanked him off etc. etc. Having put me in my place he then returned to his bedroom where he stayed for an hour, finally going outside to have a look around after he was about to leave for work anyway. I hovered around the front door waiting for him to come back in.

"Was there a plastic bag under the back wheel?"

"No," he said, mildly interested: James was always prepared to be involved in any conspiracy going.

Unfortunately, before I could ask any more, Darren slunk into the room carrying a dirty sports bag and James hustled the poor boy into the hall and out through the front door before he had a chance to say anything, although speech may have been beyond him by that stage.

"Bye-eeee," James trilled as he slammed the door shut, plastic bags and prowlers long forgotten.

I decided to go out and look for myself. There was nothing there. No hedgehog, no plastic bag, nothing. There should have been some blood on the road at least. I felt ill. No more drugs for a while. I could handle the fact that I might have imagined the freak in the tracksuit, but I was *positive* I'd run over the hedgehog...

The phone on Liz's desk rang. Maxine.

"How did you know I was sitting in Liz's seat?" I chuckled.

"It's Tracey. I need to talk to you." (Six Filipino bandits are standing over me with a machete.)

"Tracey. Sorry, I thought you were someone else."

"Who? Can I come and see you?"

"Ah –"

"I don't want to talk about it on the phone."

"Why not?"

"Can I tell you later? Who did you think it was?"

"I don't know. No one. Don't worry about it. Did you ring me on Friday night?"

"*Yes*. Thanks for ringing back."

"Sorry. I didn't want to ring you at home," I said. "It was really late."

She didn't say anything.

"What did you think of that acid anyway? Was it strong?"

No reply.

"Tracey?"

"Yes?"

"Did you have any um... hallucinations?"

"*No*. Why? Did you?"

"No, not really. I just wondered if you did."

"No, but I had an *awful* night."

She waited for me to commiserate, which I didn't.

"Well? Can I meet you for lunch today?"

"I'm quite busy today –"

"I *need* to talk to you."

Fucking hell. I barely knew the girl. I gave her directions to the office and spent the morning with the door shut drinking coffee and reading magazines and trying not to think about the man in the track-suit.

Maxine phoned through at midday and announced that Tracey had arrived and Liz was on line two. Liz kept me on the phone for twenty minutes (*calling from the Caribbean – fabulous!*) and by the time I got down to reception Tracey had already rearranged the furniture to suit herself. Mace was standing by the photocopier entranced (which to the uninitiated translated as small exclamations of wonderment as he examined the page he was photocopying); Donna Taite, the Station Manager's PA who hated women, especially good-looking ones, was bustling around sighing angrily at the fax machine; and Tracey was kneeling on the floor with Maxine, laying out pages 1-10 while Maxine did 11-20.

What band did Maxine's boyfriend play in? *Really?!* (They were completely unknown.) When were they were playing next? *Great! I'll give you my phone number.* And what size was she? *I've got a dress that would look amazing on you!*

She made a great fuss of seeing me. Everyone watched, intrigued.

As we left, Mace was smiling idiotically at us and trying to catch Tracey's eye, and Maxine called after us, "Nice to meet you Tracey. See you soon!"

"You're popular," I said as we walked to the door.

Tracey laughed. "Your hair looks good," she said.

It looked exactly the way it always did. In fact it looked worse because I'd gone to bed with it wet.

"No it doesn't."

"Yes it does," she said indignantly.

I thought we were doing some kind of Punch and Judy routine.

"You can cut the act now," I laughed. "We're nearly out."

"What do you mean?"

"I was joking."

"No you weren't." She stood there with her arms folded, refusing to go through the door.

"I was actually," I said, aware that both Maxine and Mace were still watching us. "Come on, let's have something to eat."

She pushed through the door and we walked uncomfortably along the footpath, her footsteps falling one step behind mine. I stopped when we reached the pizza place on the corner.

"Do you want to go in here?"

She hesitated but followed me in. Two men stared at her and she acknowledged the attention by adopting a friendly attitude and pirouetting into her seat.

"Sorry," she said, picking at her place mat, "I don't know what's wrong with me."

"Do you want something to eat?"

"… Alicia and I are breaking up."

"Oh?" I said. "Why's that?"

"I told her about Friday night –"

"Why did you do that?"

"Don't get mad! I didn't want to lie to her. I didn't want to hurt her."

I didn't think it necessary to point out that if she hadn't wanted to hurt her it might have been more circumspect to have said nothing.

"Is that why you rang me?"

"I wanted you to know what was going on."

"*Why?* Nothing's going on."

This seemed like a reasonable enough statement, but the effect it had on her was quite unbelievable. *Tears* came to her eyes and she pushed back her chair and walked out of the restaurant, slamming the door shut.

I nearly went after her but several people were staring accusingly at me so I ordered a pizza instead and hung around the counter examining a glass of toothpicks until it was ready.

Maxine had gone to lunch when I got back. There was a message on my desk from Tracey to phone her. I screwed it up and threw it in the bin.

She rang me an hour later, full of apologies; didn't know why she'd walked out; Alicia giving her a hard time; been off the Prozac for a few days; maybe call me later in the week?

"Prozac?" I said. "Are they still dishing that stuff out? Why are you on that?"

"Depression," she said. Then rather more ominously, "It's a long story."

I wasn't sure I wanted to hear it.

"Are you there?"

"Yeah. Sorry."

"I'll talk to you later OK? Bye bye." The bye bye bit was both childish and sexy: full of nipple-licking promise. Pity there weren't bigger breasts attached to them.

Man... How the fuck did I get involved in all this?

Dumb question.

I called James.

"Hi-eeee!"

"What's happening?"

"*Well,*" he pronounced the word perfectly before slipping back into gayboyesque. "My friend Shaun's coming around."

Shaun was sixteen and wore eyeliner to assembly.

"*And!* Martin Myers rang for you!"

James knew all about my predilection for Martin Myers. I was forever dribbling on about him. Pointing him out in magazines. (I'd started reading the sort of magazines he appeared in: *Ad Hoc* and

Advertising Monthly which Mace subscribed to.) I met him around the same time that James had moved in: Liz and I had a function to go to, one of our clients, and in a fit of bonhomie towards the new flatmate I invited James. I picked him up from the restaurant where he worked and as soon as we got there we both plucked a glass of champagne from the tray in the foyer, were each half a glass down by the time we got our name tags and simultaneously reaching for a second as we walked into the room.

It was a launch for a new car called Nu Car (*available in six exciting nu colours*), and attached to thin wires hanging from the ceiling were huge cardboard pictures of it parked on an angle on top of a mountain. A woman in futuristic white robes was walking out of the mist towards it, leading a horse by the bridle.

At one end of the room an enormous video screen had been set up. This was the payback: the presentation. The excited: *Ladies and Gentlemen, thank you. Thank you. If we could have quiet please for Reg Hanson, the Managing Director* (an air of friendly resignation whipping around the room, the audience pausing mid oyster vol-au-vent). *Good. Thank you.* (The speaker's voice – in this case Liz's – lowering and steadying, her arm reaching out to herald the arrival of this doyen of the motor trade) *Mister* – (I don't need to labour it, for we all know who he is) *Reg Hanson!* with another unnecessary attention-seeking *Ladies and Gentlemen* tagged on the end, and clap clap clapping, and Reg walking hard-faced up to the microphone, dandruff spray-painted across the neck of his expensive suit collar.

Liz then stood by the side of the makeshift stage, heaving with excitement, looking up at Reg. She'd been panicking about having to introduce him all day and had raced out at lunchtime to buy a new dress – some apricot thing that was too tight. Reg said a few weighty words: he was delighted, proud, fucking *humbled*. He actually said: *You know.* (Stop whilst audience digest this. Give them time. Give them time.) *It's a very humbling experience to be involved with...* blah blah blah, and then casting around confidently like a man used to having his orders obeyed by an assembly line of Pauls and Daves and Debbies, he cued the video package and the lights obediently went down and the car zipped along mountain roads, through forests and over fiords, the woman in the robes at the helm, sexily checking the rear-view mirror every now and then.

Where's the horse? I yelled out halfway through it, which set James off and he started doing his face at me (a gay interpretation of Munch's *The Scream*, basically). Liz looked over at us and mouthed *Shh!* and turned back to the screen, pencil sharpened, and the guy standing next to her laughed and looked at me. I willed him to turn around again but he didn't.

And now... until the end of the evening... *Track* the object of your desire throughout the room without them noticing! *Stand* somewhere where they can see you! *Watch* as they queue for the buffet! *Smile!* Even if they're not looking! That sort of palaver. Exhausting in its execution, and often disappointing. Especially if you risk it and go to the toilet and when you come back they're... they've... gone.

When the presentation finished and the lights came up, James deflected the disapproving looks by deftly picking up a Nu Car brochure and examining it while I nodded fuzzily at the pictures. Liz came over, leaving what's-his-name to drift off untethered into the crowd.

"That was good," I said loudly as she steamed up to us.

"Hello," James said, putting out his hand, "I'm James."

This diverted her attention for a moment: she'd been about to do her *I expect more* speech, but shook his hand instead, "Liz Bailey. Public Relations."

"Oh yes," said James, adopting a businessman's air, "and you're Ruth's boss?"

"That's right," she said brusquely (having looked at his name tag and noting that he was of no importance to her whatsoever). "Excuse me won't you?" She looked over at Reg and turned back to smile at James, just in case. "Nice to meet you," she added insincerely and started to walk off. I grabbed her arm.

"Liz. Who was that standing next to you?"

She looked impatiently at me and then decided to tell me. "Martin Myers. The director."

"Did he do the ad?"

She nodded. "He's hot," she said, and walked off.

Liz always managed to be at least two decades behind the rest of world in most things, ad lingo included. She used words like *hot* and *happening* like they were. It didn't seem to have any detrimental effect on her career. In fact she would have made a good prostitute if she hadn't been in PR because fundamentally PR was just metaphorical cock sucking, and Liz would have gone down on anything if the price was right.

She was fiddling around inside Reg Hanson's trousers now.

"Did you see that guy next to Liz?" I asked James.

"*No*. What guy?"

"Martin someone. The director. With Liz. He was gorgeous."

"After you," he said and walked into me, spilling his champagne over me in his haste to be first.

We spotted him at the bar. He was standing by himself and we checked him out for a few minutes in case I'd made a mistake. Nope. He was skinny with dark brown hair, wearing a battered green shirt with a button-down collar, black sixties trousers and black shoes. They looked like his going-out clothes, pulled out of a canvas kitbag that smelled of kerosene lanterns and cold salt water.

James walked straight up to him and said, "Hi-eeee, I'm James," and stood there grinning at him like a gay idiot. "And you're – ?"

"Martin," he replied, smiling, "and you're – ?"

"Ruth," I said.

"*Root?*" he laughed. I checked his eyes.

"*Ruth*," I said, every inch the charmed schoolma'am. "And you're on – ?"

"What do you mean?" he said and laughed.

"You're the director?" James said.

"Yeah."

"Did you do tonight's ad?" I asked.

"Yeah." He laughed again. Definitely on the scenic route.

"I have to go," he said and walked off, turning back and smiling at us. "To dinner."

"Where are you going?" James hurried after him while I stayed at the bar and watched while James joked and giggled with him at the door and got him to write his phone number down. Before he left he looked over at me and smiled. I spent the rest of the evening happily drunk, ignited by this smile, hugging it to me like a hot-water bottle on a cold night.

He rang the flat a few days later saying that James had told him to ring if he wanted anything. I laughed. I had some coke so I offered to drop it round, spending ages deciding what to wear and getting lost on the way there, arriving just as he was about to go out. There was a taxi waiting for him downstairs so I only had time to give him the coke and get the money before he had to go. It took me hours to get home again but I didn't care: I was besotted. Martin Myers! And now he'd just rung. Again!

"What did he want?" I said to James, excitedly filling in the smiley faces Liz had drawn on her pad.

"He wants you to ring him."

"Really? Thanks James, bye-eeee."

"Bye love, give that lovely cock a squeeze for me."

"Yeah, sure," I snorted. "Not much chance of that."

"Send him over here then. Bye-eeee."

I put down the phone and called him immediately.

"Did you want me for something?" I said in my Maxine voice.

Major turn-off in the Martin department. There was a moment's silence and then he said, "Yeah. I was ringing to see if you had any –"

"Oh right. I can drop it off if you like."

"I can come –"

"No, no, I don't mind. What time?"

We arranged to meet at his flat at seven and he hung up, *annoyed?* *Shit.* I got my bag and went down to reception.

"How was lunch?" Maxine asked, her eyes widening.

"Good thanks."

"How do you know Tracey? She's really nice."

"And I'm not?"

"I didn't say *that!*"

"Yeah, well, If Liz calls, I've gone out."

"Where are you going?"

"I'm going *out.* If that's all right with you," I said, and realised with a start that I'd never actually been *rude* to Maxine before. Tracksuit Man must have really rattled me, although by then I was putting it down to the late night and the acid and a versatile imagination. It was the fact that Tracey had wooed Maxine so successfully that annoyed me. Maxine was *mine.* She was my friend, not Tracey's. She worked at *my* work, and she took messages for *me,* and that somehow made her *my* property.

It was only later that I realised that this was just the beginning of Tracey's diligent assimilation into *my* life.

5: A tablespoon of warm sperm

The Valium seems to be doing the trick. I've just been getting up every day and sitting at the kitchen table and writing this. I've been out to the shops a few times, and today I went to the library and got a book on how to write, and one on grammar. The first one's about *the welding together of the various ingredients into a well-constructed whole, and the value of advance planning*. Advance planning? None of this would have happened if there'd been any *advance planning* going on. Then it goes on about having to have *a sense of place*. That unless you've got a sense of place none of it will have any relevance to the reader. I'm trying to *eliminate* a sense of place, not fucking highlight it. I don't want anybody to know where I am, or who I am for that matter: only the bare essentials anyway. Not that I've done it properly, I know that. It's almost impossible to *disguise* a sense of place. The minute you start describing it, people work it out. As for Ruth, it's a common enough name. I looked it up in one of those baby books once and it said: "Hebrew. The meaning is uncertain." So, even my name doesn't have any meaning. Why doesn't that surprise me?

The other one's like a reference book: it explains what verbs and past participles are and then tells you off for including *actually* and *really* and *definitely* anywhere in your writing. For example, you mustn't say "it was *really* big", when you could just say "it was big". That threw me. Why say it was big when you could say it was *really* big? Typical. Can't even follow a few simple instructions on how to write.

There's no atlas at home so while I was at the library I tried to find out about that picture I've got on the wall, of the house with the windows. There are several San Juans: one's on the island of Puerto Rico, and there's a San Juan *lake*, I think it was, in Utah; maybe this is that one because it says in the magazine article something about not minding doing the dishes with a view of the Rocky Mountains. I could have sworn it was the sea – a lake seems disappointingly hemmed in, confined.

I feel like that myself, but I have one Valium at ten o'clock and another in the afternoon at about four, which keeps the lid on everything. For the moment...

After I left work that day I went shopping. I bought a new dress and some clingy black boots and then walked purposefully towards where I knew there was a sex shop and walked straight in and started browsing through the racks. It wasn't as bad as I thought it was going to be: the man behind the counter took no notice of me at all, he was too busy working on a dildo display. I bought a rubber camisole with holes cut out for the nipples and one of the strap-on dildos. It wasn't the biggest one they had – I thought about buying that as a present for James (but even then it probably wouldn't have touched the sides).

It took me a while to figure out what James did with a dildo when he was by himself. It was obvious, but for some reason I didn't twig for months. Not until I was sitting on the edge of his bed one morning while he was having a cup of tea and there was a blowfly zooming around the carpet. I looked down and it had landed on this enormous poo-covered dildo poking out from under his bed. When I asked him who had been there he smiled and said *no one*.

Freak.

I didn't go near his room for weeks.

I thought the dildo would do for Tracey when I saw her next. Pity I couldn't have found some use for it with Martin Myers, but I was still in two minds as to whether he was gay or not. He definitely had a feminine air about him, although I'd caught him looking at my breasts when I went round there that first time. But then gayboys did that – took a quick look at everything. They were still men, after all. James had come to the happy conclusion that Martin was a closet queen. It was only a matter of time he said, eyes staring off into the middle distance as he pictured Martin Myers striding down the hall to his bedroom.

I didn't bother going back to work: I went to a bar and had a glass of wine. Two more and I'd changed into my new clothes in the toilets, including the rubber thing, which felt OK once it had warmed up a bit. You couldn't tell I had it on by looking at the dress, although you could definitely see the outline of my nipples. I bought a bottle of champagne to take to Martin's, banging into the bumper of the car in front of me as I drove off.

Martin lived in a flat above a cycle shop. That first time I went there I parked directly opposite and as I got out of the car I looked up and saw him standing at the window. He was waiting for the cab, not me, but at the time it was excruciating: I felt like I'd forgotten how to walk properly; I even caught myself trying to whistle. By the time I'd rung the buzzer and he'd opened the door I was beside myself, blushing and bellowing hello at him. So this time I parked two streets away and walked back so he wouldn't see me arriving. He answered the door with a distracted hello.

"Good. I'm good," I said. (Not that he'd asked.) "How are you? Here's something to drinks. *Drink*."

"Thanks. Come in." He bounded up the stairs in front of me.

His flat was small with low ceilings and strange corners, like a ship's hold; the walls were painted white and he had several abstract paintings stretched over canvas and hung around the room. A huge TV dominated one corner and dozens of videos and CDs were scattered on the floor around it. A shot of Cleopatra holding an icecream was pausing on the TV screen, and there was an open storyboard pad on the table.

"How are you?" I said, walking into the edge of the table. "*Ow*. Is this what you're working on?"

"Are you all right?"

"Yeah." I rubbed my shin bone. "I went to a sex shop this afternoon."

"Shall we have a drink first?" He laughed and went to get some glasses from the kitchen. I ripped the foil off the top of the bottle and the cork rocketed towards the ceiling, wondering what the occasion was. I poured him a glass.

"Thanks. I've got an edit shift at eight."

An hour. Fuck.

"That's all right. I've got some coke."

"Great," he said, glancing at my dress.

Suddenly the concept of sticky-out nipples didn't seem like such a good idea. "You don't have a jumper do you?"

"A jumper?" He smiled.

"Yeah. I'm a bit cold."

He went to his bedroom and came back with a black coat.

"Is this all right?"

"Great. Wonderful. Thanks." I put it on quickly before he could take it back, noting the smell of it. It was wonderful. I felt wonderful in it. We sat down at the table and he watched as I cut out two lines and began to rip up the cover of a magazine to make a tube to snort it with.

"Shit," he muttered, knocking over his glass as he grabbed for the magazine. He jumped up and his chair went flying backwards.

"Sorry. *Shit*," I said. "Have you got a cloth?"

"*Fuck*," he said, wiping at his wet trousers, champagne running off the edge of the table and onto the floor. "I borrowed that from a guy at work, that's all."

I looked at the table. The coke had been swamped in champagne and his storyboard was all wet.

"My storyboard," he said, shaking the liquid off it. He got a cloth and mopped up the mess while I straightened piles and moved things around.

"I'm sorry. That was my fault," I said, handing him the coke. "You can have that."

"No, that's OK."

"Please. I'd like you to."

"No, I'd prefer to pay for it."

"*Please.*"

He didn't answer but poured himself another glass of champagne while I chopped out two more lines. I snorted my line, sniff, snuffle, snort. He looked at his watch and then sucked up his coke in one competent hit.

"I've got to get my tapes organised. Thanks for bringing that round. How much do I owe you?"

"That's OK. Where are you going?"

"... Digi One."

"Would you mind if I came?"

"Ah..." he said, getting up and filling a shoulder bag with tapes.

"I promise I won't try and leap on you," I said.

Why did I say that?

He laughed. "It's not that. Would you want to come?"

Rhetorical question. Pointedly ignored.

"Might as well. We could go in my car," I said.

"I'll be there most of the night."

"I don't mind. It'll be interesting."

He zipped up his bag, not looking at me. "Sure."

I assumed this meant I could go. I hoped he wasn't going to ask for his coat back. I buttoned it up while he got the rest of his things and we went downstairs to the car. I drove to Digi One keeping up a steady babble, trying not to let him see that I was covering my right eye every now and then to stop there being two of everything in front of me.

Digi One had a discreet neon over the door and a night buzzer. We were ushered into a darkened room with heavy drapes, and what looked like an oversized computer in the corner, by an impassive girl in capri pants who blinked when I asked her if they had a toilet and announced that Sebastian was our editor, it was Indonesian on the menu tonight and – direct eye contact with Martin, the tip of her tongue touching her pink frosted top lip – *and I'm Lorna.*

Sebastian sat poised at the editing desk and then spun around casually to greet us. Perfect timing. He had red pudgy lips and a silver bracelet.

"Hello." He smiled professionally. "I'm Sebastian. Help yourselves to a drink."

Lorna took her cue and gave us a guided tour of the fridge which was beside itself with alcohol and freshly squeezed orange juice, and then the side table which sported a matching white tea set and a big white plate with chocolate biscuits fanned artistically around the edge. She would get us coffee. She frowned when she came to an enormous glass fruit bowl which had two apples in the bottom of it.

"Unbelievable," she said, looking at Sebastian. "I'll show you where the toilets are," she covered, and led me to to a vast fluorescent chamber full of flowers and free tampons.

I couldn't undo the domes on the rubber thing, and by the time I'd got back Martin and Sebastian had started. The fruit bowl had been replaced with one overflowing with grapes, bananas, kiwi fruit and plums. Lychees and star fruit. Martin was drinking a beer so I helped myself to a half bottle of champagne from the fridge and sank into the leather couch.

I don't like to remember what happened next. (I found out later that this wasn't *all* that happened next, but it was all that I remembered.)

What happened next was that I proceeded to drink myself into a stupor while they tried that shot again, or took two frames off here, or tried a cut rather than a fade, and after I'd got the hang of it I took Martin's coat off and put my feet up on the couch and *started to argue with them* about which take was better, or which shot worked best. Sebastian didn't seem to mind but Martin frowned and sniffed and finally snapped at me to *be quiet please*. Somewhere along the way an Indonesian banquet happened but I just kept on hoeing into the free booze and managed to get another line off Martin before announcing that I'd bought a strap-on dildo in a sex shop. Martin ignored me. Sebastian looked at my crotch. I must have passed out after that because next thing, Sebastian was waking me up saying Martin had gone home, but how about a drink? There was a bit of shit going down with his girlfriend but that dildo sounds amazing. He sat down next to me on the couch and put one arm around me and his other hand straight up my dress. *And I let him.*

I even helped him. I took off my dress and he almost came when he saw the rubber outfit. I yanked open the domes for him and he unzipped his jeans and knelt by the couch urgently wanking himself while he put two fingers inside me. It was revolting.

But that didn't stop me. I wriggled around on his fingers moaning *"Harder, harder"*, and watched his face *uh uh uh* while he came; a tablespoon of warm sperm spurting onto my bare leg.

I woke up at five the next morning with a raging hangover. I was naked. Sebastian was in my bed. Fuck. *Fuck.*

What was happening to me?

Drunk. Not just drunk, *paralytic.* Drugs. Sex with all and sundry. And even going into a sex shop. I'd never been in one before in my life. And then that fucking freak by my car. Weird shit. All this had started happening since I moved in with James. Maybe living with James had desensitised me. That must be it... James's behaviour was rubbing off on me. It was time to straighten up. I looked nervously at Sebastian.

Well overdue.

6: Emerald budgies

"Great flocks of emerald budgies are flying through your brain," Tracey said, reading the horoscopes in the paper. "Sorry."

"Pardon?"

"That's what it says here. Great flocks of emerald budgies are flying through your brain."

"Yes, but what does it mean?"

"*I don't know*. That's what it says here!"

It was Friday morning. I'd rung Maxine and told her I was feeling sick and wasn't coming in. Half an hour later Tracey was on the phone offering to come over, taking down the address before I could think of an excuse why not. She arrived wearing white jeans and huge biker boots and carrying a plastic bag of fruit. James had the morning off and pranced around behaving as if she'd just delivered him up a bunch of ripe twelve-year-olds, and then took himself off to the kitchen to make fruit milkshakes. Tracey took a cursory look around the flat, boot buckles clinking and clunking, and then settled herself on the couch to read the paper. I was reading my book.

I didn't want her to be there: I was planning on doing my washing and cleaning out the car. I'd been keeping a low profile all week – just coming home from work and going to bed. It had taken me the entire week to get over my hangover, compounded as it was with guilt and remorse, guilt and remorse, *guilt guilt guilt*.

– Why did I do that? What a fucking *idiot*.

– Look, just forget it. There's nothing you can do about it now. People do worse things.

– Do they? *Do they really?*

– Look, stop fucking flagellating yourself. At least you didn't murder anybody.

– Yeah well I might as well have.

I hadn't heard a thing from Martin; Sebastian had phoned three times and left throaty messages on the answerphone, and now Tracey was the last person I wanted to see. Deliver us from temptation for thine is the glory et cetera.

James swept in with the drinks on a tray and tripped over my slippers. Milk slurped out of the glasses and onto the carpet and he bustled around like somebody's mother, soaking up the milk with a towel and then throwing the towel into the corner beside the couch. It was all too much. I gave up. Might as well get stoned.

"Let's have some hash shall we?"

"Yaaaayyyy," said James. He'd been fretting about my good girliness all week; if I was as bad as him it didn't make him feel so bad. "*Yaaaayyyy!*" he repeated, making a face at Tracey, who laughed. He busied himself putting on some music and finding his pipe and getting the hash ready.

"So," I said, endeavouring to get into the spirit of things. "How are you, Tracey?"

"OK…"

She was standing by the heater glancing at the backs of her legs. She took a tissue out of her pocket and examined it carefully as she unfolded it.

"Alicia wants me to move out."

I went back to the book I'd been reading.

"Don't you want to know why?" she demanded.

"I know why. Why?"

"Because of you – because of… us."

"*What?* Because we went out?'

'Yeah, and because we – you know –"

James looked up from his ministrations like an interested fox terrier.

"What? Because we – *what?*"

"You know what I mean," she said, twisting the tissue in her hands.

"No I don't."

"James." She looked at him plaintively. "Is she always like this?"

"Nothing to do with me love," James said, handing her the pipe. "Most of the time."

"Don't be horrid," she said to me. And then matter-of-factly to James, "Have you got any matches?"

"There you go love."

"Thanks love."

She lit the pipe, smiling at him.

I was horrid. I couldn't help myself. There was something about her that didn't add up. She made me want to tie her up and spank her.

So much for cleaning the car.

"Sorry," I said. "I'm just tired."

James squealed.

"I *am*."

I had some hash and went and got a bucket from the kitchen.

"What are you *doing?*" Tracey asked when I came back.

"Cleaning the bathroom."

James stirred his milkshake busily.

"But I've come to visit you."

"You can help if you want."

I was only able to deliver short messages by this stage: I had to keep moving.

Her face dropped.

"Stay here then."

She scrambled after me and looked over my shoulder affectionately as I stood in the bathroom doorway. It looked like a two-hour job. The walls were filthy, thick with the ghosts of gayboys past: the casual splatterings of shaving foam and hair mousse; the squirts of eye wash; the trails of toothpaste; the nose pickings and the blackheads. And, always, ever present, gathered along skirting boards and knitted together in the corners with dust and scraps of toilet paper, the *hair*.

"What do you want me to do?" she asked. Her breath smelt.

"The bathroom cabinet?"

"We don't have to." Her chin rested suggestively on my shoulder.

"I'm going to," I said.

"Why?"

"You don't have to help. I can do it by myself. You go back to the lounge and talk to James."

"I don't want to go back to the lounge and talk to James. I want to talk to you."

"I don't mind if you go back to the lounge."

"I want to stay here."

"OK, well you do the bathroom cabinet then."

I filled the bucket with hot water while Tracey got on her knees and surveyed the contents of the bathroom cabinet.

"*Yuk,*" she said.

"You don't have to do it."

"I know," she said crossly, reaching in and picking out two used corn plasters, a sock, and a handful of disposable razors clogged with hair. Several strings of dental floss, coated intermittently with blood and yellow feculence (tossed in there by James, who maintained a rigid biweekly regime of teeth cleaning and dental flossing) completed this unsavoury line-up, which she placed in a little pile on the floor. Meanwhile I was having my own sordid relationship with the sink, last date cleaned unknown.

I was too stoned to talk: my ears were ringing and I kept turning the taps on and off so I wouldn't have to say anything. I concentrated on scraping the black mould from the base of the hot tap.

Tracey stood up, wiping her hands on her jeans, and looked out the window.

"Oh look! Here puss puss puss puss!" she said and took off outside.

Obviously a cat. I finished cleaning the sink and looked out the window to see her mashing a black kitten against her sternum. She kissed the top of its head and held it up to the window to show me before coming back inside.

"*Loook,*" she said, standing in the bathroom doorway with the shocked kitten swinging by its neck between her fingers. "Can we keep it? *I* could keep it," she corrected herself.

"Where did it come from?" I hadn't seen any cats or kittens around the place. I'd looked once or twice.

"It's lost. I'm going to show it to James."

"You haven't finished here yet."

"I know," she said. "It's your bathroom." She rushed off and I followed her into the lounge, cloth in hand.

James was sitting on the couch holding his breath in an exaggerated fashion.

"James, this is Polly."

"*Polly?*" I said.

She didn't answer but stroked the kitten's head vigorously, the pink lining of its lids revealed as she pulled the skin back in hefty strokes.

James's eyes bulged as he held on for the last vestige of chemical enhancement before exploding smoke and spit into the air and going into a death-defying coughing fit. The kitten *riaowed* and twisted itself out of Tracey's hand. It landed with a tiny thud on the carpet and flew under the armchair.

"Polly," Tracey called, on her hands and knees. "Here Pols."

Pols? For fuck's sake. I went back to the bathroom and started on the shower. The music stopped and I could hear Tracey trying unsuccessfully to coax the kitten out from beneath the armchair. James was on the phone arranging his drugs for the night: "Yes, that's it – ten. They're not *all* for me love. What? You think they *are?*" General hooting and yowling, followed by the supposedly cryptic financial arrangements in case the drug squad were listening in. Tracey came into the bathroom.

"Can you help me get the cat out?"

"Just leave it. It'll come out when it wants to."

"It wants to come out now."

"It'll be all right where it is."

"No it won't."

"It will."

"*It won't.*"

"Oh for goodness sake." I stood up.

"No, no, forget it," she said and flounced out of the bathroom.

I controlled the urge to run after her and put her in her room and turned my attention to the toilet which was beginning to smell like a public urinal. (James liked the smell: the redolence of happy orgasm achieved with one's cock poking through a hole in the wall, listening to the desperate slurping from the next cubicle, smacking one's hips against the particle board, the plywood, the formica: take that you cunt, take that you bastard. Or crouched, an anonymous penis rammed down his throat, pulling himself off to the tune of the filling cistern, his debasement welcome and complete.)

I looked in the bowl. I knew what was in there – it had been there for over a week: a brown splattering cemented to the rim of the bowl. The rim. How do you get shit on the rim of a toilet bowl? The rubber gloves were in the kitchen but I'd have to walk past the lounge to get there. Maybe Tracey had gone home: I couldn't hear any noises coming from the lounge.

Too bad. I didn't like her that much anyway. Come to think of it, I knew fuck all about her, except the stuff we'd talked about the night we went out. Her parents were divorced and her mother had remarried some guy called Gordon who had two daughters, one of whom Tracey had done it with on Christmas Day while the others were out taking the dog for a walk. (I knew quite a bit about *this*.) The daughter's name was Alison and she drove a company car, had matching floral suitcases, and was about to get married to Brian. Tracey had phoned her after Christmas to say hello but she was tied up in a meeting for the rest of her life, but she'd see Tracey at the wedding. Something like that. What else? Decided she was gay at fourteen when she kept wanting to bury her face in the back of her best friend's long brown hair; sneaked out to a gay club at sixteen and got picked up by a woman who was ten years older than her, had particularly wonderful sex with said dyke: fate sealed. She was now twenty-four, intermittently on old-world anti-depressants, wanted to be famous and had no tits. Seemed to like me. Was, however, shaping up to be moody, uptight and competitive, but reasonably pliable in the sex department. Very pliable actually, if you could be bothered working your way through the rest of the shit. Maybe I should persuade her to get her nipples pierced and I could put a chain through them and pull her along behind me, naked, at gay marches. Good *idea*, Ruth.

I left the toilet and went off in search of her. The house was empty: I found her and James in the garden out the back. Tracey was cutting up a cardboard box.

"For the cat," James explained, stabbing ineffectively at the lawn with a trowel. James cultivated this type of stupidity: being thought of as useless was in no way offensive to him – he had other, bigger fish to fry.

"I'm going to take it home," Tracey said. "We haven't got a gar-den." She took the trowel off James who looked relieved and went inside.

I followed the curve of her waist down as she knelt with her back to me, digging up dirt and dumping it enthusiastically in the box. "What about Alicia?" I said. "What are you going to do?"

"I don't know. Move out."

"Where will you go?"

"I don't know. My mother's."

"Will that be OK?"

"Probably not."

"Is there anything I can do?" I asked, my eyes roaming around her bottom.

"Like what?" She turned around and smiled.

"I don't know. Kiss you."

"All right," she said, dropping the trowel. She got to her feet and began to kiss me fervently on the lips. Several neighbours would be rooted to the spot: the only trouble was that I was on the wrong drugs – hashish and public displays of homosexual affection weren't a particularly happy mix for me.

"Let's go inside," I said, trying to twist my head away.

"No, let's stay here," she said and kissed me again.

If I hadn't have been so stoned I probably would have enjoyed it, but as it was my face felt like it was about to explode, and her mouth with its probing tongue became a departure lounge of hot bacilli jumping off the fleshy concourse.

She sucked my top lip vigorously and let me go. "Did you like that?" she smiled.

"Yeah, it was OK," I mumbled. "Coffee?"

"*Please.*" She turned back to the garden and began to dig boisterously, dirt flying everywhere. "You make it and I'll finish this. Get Polly out from under the chair," she ordered as I frogmarched myself inside.

The balance of power appeared to have shifted.

James was comatose on the couch scratching at his groin.

"Itchy," he said and farted.

I went to the kitchen and put the kettle on.

"Cat," James said.

"*What?*" He was beginning to get on my nerves.

I took the coffee in. The kitten was sniffing at the newspaper in the middle of the floor. We both watched as it reversed onto its haunches and twitched its pelvis at us. A watery black coil crept onto the carpet next to the front page.

"Good girl!" Tracey said, coming in the door carrying the dirt box. The kitten licked its anus and then looked at it, startled (*bloody hell*), before skittling back under the armchair.

There was a high-pitched ringing in my ears which disoriented me. I was suddenly in the mood for nothing to happen. I stood there in silhouette while lightning bolted between clouds and the wicked witch laughed into her mirror at me. Ya ha ha ha ha! I felt formless –

like a woman used to wearing corsets and finding they were all in the wash. Like my entire life was a waste of time, which in fact it was. And whose wasn't? We were all just providing a service, no matter who we were: we were all propping each other up. Or ourselves. Human symbiosis. What a complete waste of fucking time. I needed Tracey to confirm my own desirability to myself; Tracey needed me... for what?

"I'll give you a ride home," I said and went and got my car keys.

"But we haven't had our coffee yet," she said when I came back. "And you didn't drink your milkshake."

"Never mind," I said wearily. "You have your coffee while James finds a box for the cat –"

James looked at me, perplexed. A *box?*

"– And I'll get the cat out from under the chair." I got on my knees and grabbed the cat around its soft belly. Extracting its claws from my wrist, I presented it to Tracey. "There you go."

She took the cat and stood there sulkily, patting it. James didn't look like making any signs of moving, so I was about to get a box myself when Tracey made emphatic eye contact with me, indicating that I was to go into the kitchen.

"I don't want to go home," she said when we got there.

"Eh?"

"I didn't say I wanted to go home."

"What?" I closed the door.

"Are you trying to get rid of me?"

"No. I'm tired, that's all."

"Why did you bother with me in the first place?"

"What are you talking about?"

"Well, why did you want to have a relationship with me?"

"I didn't say I wanted to have a relationship with you."

"*Yes you did.*" She looked down at the cat who was now purring, beginning to enjoy all the attention.

"When did I say that?"

"You said –"

"What?"

"I'm not going to tell you if you don't remember."

"Go on."

"No."

"Go *on*. What did I say?"

"You said you loved me," she blurted out and then stared at me.

"Did I?"

(I couldn't remember. Knowing me I probably did.)

She looked at me disbelievingly and walked out. I waited in the kitchen until I heard her go out the front door and then followed her outside. She was waiting by the car. I unlocked her door and then put the dirt box in the boot. She didn't talk to me at all on the way home, but sniffed and peeped in at the kitten constantly, wagging a finger at it and saying *hello*, and then looking out the window intently. When we finally turned into her street she said, "Park out the front. Alicia's not here."

There was no room to park so I pulled up alongside a car directly in front of her house, turning to look at her with a forced *there you go* expression.

"Are you coming in?"

"It's OK." I just wanted to go home and clean up my room. Fold washing. Pick lint off my socks. Kill myself.

"Come and see where I live." Her head wilted in deference to the Omnipotent Subjugator. *"Please."*

I couldn't be bothered arguing: I found a space and followed her into her flat carrying the dirt box. Two women were sitting at the kitchen table smoking.

"Hey fuck – Trace," one said, eyeing me like carrion.

"Hi-eeee," said Tracey, sounding disturbingly like James. "This is Sarah and Debbie. This is my friend Ruth."

"Hello," I said.

They nodded and watched me as I followed Tracey down the hall. The flat was a shrine to not giving a shit. Huge streaky paintings of nude women covered entire walls, badly welded sculptures were draped in garments, and old furniture propped up books and vases and mirrors and teapots; there were plastic flowers and tinsel Sellotaped to walls, torn carpets, decaying armchairs, bulging ashtrays. Her room – their room – jangled and glittered and chimed. Tangled piles of clothes covered the floor and I tripped on something and accidentally top-dressed the heap of clothes nearest me with dirt from the cat box. It was too much to take in. I wanted to be in a big white room with a billowing white curtain and a white vase of white flowers.

Tracey plonked herself down on the bed with the cat. She patted the bed, "Come and sit here."

"I'd better go." I looked around for somewhere to put the box and balanced it on an armchair that had a grubby computer sitting on it.

"Please. Just for a second."

I sat next to her and she put her arm around me and pulled my head into her neck.

"Poor you," she said.

I was thinking much the same thing, my nose bending painfully into her jugular.

"It's all too much isn't it?"

"Yeah." She didn't know the half of it. "I'd better get going," I said, and stood up.

She didn't look at me but stroked the kitten furiously.

"Bye then," I said at the bedroom door. "Thanks for the fruit."

"That's OK," she said quietly.

I managed to get out of the house without bumping into anybody and drove home. James had gone to work. The cat shit was setting nicely on the carpet and the heater was on full. I picked up the newspaper and lay on my bed reading the horoscopes. Great flocks of emerald budgies weren't just flying through my brain – they were *roosting there*. Squawking, shitting, eating – laying eggs.

I crawled under the covers and my foot touched something clammy where the sheet tucked into the mattress. I gripped it with my toes and winched it out. It was the rubber camisole. As I tried to chuck it over the side of the bed it wrapped around my hand and flicked back and slapped me in the face.

I dreamt that Tracey was Tracksuit Man, her hair thinning and her face melding into his. He was balancing a big book in his moth-eaten hands, rocking backwards and forwards on his heels intoning the names of all the animals I'd *murdered* over the years, each had a name, each had a spirit, and while he talked he became her, he became blonde and petulant and she gripped my wrist and droned on about lesbians and love, each had a soul, each had a spirit, and she became him became her became him begat her

I woke sometime later and drove up to the shops and got a packet of biscuits and some chips and ate them in the car on the way home, then went back to bed.

7: What I was playing at

The next morning I got up and made some tea and stood in the doorway of my bedroom drinking it. My room was a tip. No wonder I felt depressed. I put the rubber camisole and the dildo into a rubbish sack and stuffed it under the bed. The sun was coming out in fits and starts, shining lightly through the bedroom window. It looked pretty enough to start with but as I flung sheets around and picked up socks and shook newspapers and examined hair (not all of it mine – *so whose was it then?*), thousands of dust particles began to gather and float haphazardly around the room until I was surrounded on all sides by them. I stood still and breathed slowly through my mouth. I was a giant woman wreaking havoc in the galaxy: worlds shot forward like pellets. I closed the blind. This subtext of human waste always disturbed me – I knew it was there, but I didn't want to see it. Like a lot of shit in my life.

There was my rapidly deteriorating mental health for a start. I decided to make a list of my behaviour pre- and post-James to see if I could confirm my osmosis theory. I hoped Tracey would leave me alone now: it didn't matter how good-looking she was, the chemical mix wasn't right. I didn't like her smell. And anyway, the beauty thing was a complete joke. Plain women didn't have choices, did they? Women with huge squashy noses or faces like avocados couldn't pick and choose who they went out with; they had to make do. (Unless they were rich.) And, yep, here it came, wriggling out of the recesses of my tiny brain, the chant of the hopeful: *Or had a great personality*. That was bullshit as well. Ugly women with great personalities weren't in such big demand. And what happened if you got a double whammy: ugly as fuck *and* dreary? What then?

Next please.

Shallow as fuck. That was me. Attracted to people because of their looks, and then finding out I didn't like them much – because of their looks. Because they'd been cosseted and cooed over for entire life-times, most of them. And sometimes the opposite: the gorgeous co-dependants clinging to loud-mouths and junkies and makeshift daddies, cowards clinging to bullies; people-pleasers ready to betray you at a moment's notice if it meant a safer harbour; women who had learned to protect themselves in childhood from the pain of discour-agement, from being told they weren't good enough; little girls who vowed to be good, to please their keepers, to avoid anything nasty – all at the expense of being aware of how other people might feel. (And though they appeared to be helpful, they weren't concerned at all with the welfare of others: they were merely concerned with being 'good', with how others *saw them*, demanding others to move towards them on their own terms, never quite sure if they would be able to hold their position.) Constraint, uncertainty, vulnerability. Oh how I loved those qualities! These were the women who fascinated me most: the beautiful, shop-soiled ones – but I foolishly imbued all ruby-lipped, picture-postcard women with qualities such as *enigmatic*, *artistic*, *delightfully vague*, or whatever, if their eyes so much as glazed over, but if it was somebody ugly I'd think… nothing. I probably wouldn't even notice that their eyes had glazed over, so busy would I be peering over their shoulder.

Pity I hadn't thought about that a little earlier in the day. Tracey was beautiful, no doubt about it, but whenever I was in her company I could hear the faint wailing of sirens somewhere way off in the dis-tance. I just hadn't worked out what was on fire yet.

She phoned just as I got out of the shower. She was calling from a phone box and there was some problem with the line, so I pretended I couldn't hear her, hell-*low*ed a couple of times in a jokey American accent, and hung up.

James answered it the second time, emerging from his bedroom at the last minute in a pair of greying Y-fronts ballooning in the bottom area. I stood there waving *no no* at him but he looked right through me and croaked *here she is love, see you soon love, bye love* and passed me the phone.

"It's Tracey."

"Was it you who called before?"

"*Yes*. What are you doing?"

"Nothing. I've just got up."

"Do you want to come to Alison's wedding with me? It's next week."

"Who's Alison?"

"*I told you.*" (Violent unexpected wind shift. Storm jib ready.)

"Did you? Sorry. Where are you?"

"In a phone box."

"Why aren't you at home?"

"Alicia didn't come home last night. She stayed at Rose's."

"Who's Rose?"

"Her old girlfriend. They came back this morning. We had a big fight." She sounded like she was going to start crying again.

I knew she wanted me to ask her to come round – but if I did I'd be well and truly implicated. Still, I had to do something (*help other people every day, especially those at home*) so I went for the soft option.

"This wedding, can I call you back and let you know?"

"I'll be at my mother's," she said accusingly.

"Why don't you give me a call during the week? Listen Tracey, the kettle's boiling. I've got to go. Give me a call at work on Monday, OK?"

"*What*, you're not going *now*?"

I'd never met anyone who could be so offended at the merest rebuff, the tiniest insult.

"What? Shit, it's boiling, I'd better get it. Seeya. Seeya Tracey."

"I can't believe you're hanging up on me!"

"I'm not. Look I've got to go. Talk to you soon."

"*Ruth!* Please don't hang up on me!"

"I'm not, OK? Call me at work." I put the phone down. It rang again.

"That was *so mean*," she said. "How could you do that?"

"Do what? Sorry. I've turned it off now."

"*You've turned what off now?!*" she screamed.

"The kettle, calm down."

"Can I come over and see you?" she said in a tiny, suicidal voice.

"I'm going out. Why don't you come over one night during the week?"

She slammed the phone down.

James came back from the kitchen with a piece of toast loaded with peanut butter in one hand, scratching his groin with the other.

"How do you know if you've got crabs?" he asked, munching his toast. "I think I've seen something." He stood by the fireplace in his underpants looking at me ingenuously, a dribble of butter running down his chin.

"God, you're disgusting," I said. "That's revolting." I went to my room. Jesus. They could be crawling all over the toilet seat... Or hopping. I had to find a new flat; I had to write my list as well – James's behaviour wasn't just affecting me, it was bloody well *infecting* me.

James poked his head around the door. "Are you all right?" he said, coming in.

"No, I'm not actually, and would you mind putting some trousers on? *Don't* sit on the bed James!"

He jumped up.

"I don't want crabs on my bed thanks."

"No," he said, looking at me pensively. "Do you think I should I go to the chemist?"

"*I don't know.* What do you *think* you should do?"

"Don't get shitty with me love just because you're having girl-friend problems."

"James, go away."

He farted and left the room, verminous Y-fronts disappearing around the door after him.

What a shit little life I was leading. I got a pen and paper and sat on the bed writing up the *Ruth Life Map: Recent Experiences:*

> Dealing drugs
> Drinking
> Seeing things (?)
> Sex – Sebastian

I read it back: it looked like the obscure offspring of a dull poem written by one of those fifty-year-old women who suddenly get famous writing about babies they had thirty years ago and sex they had last night with a 'horny' literary agent. You knelt with your manhood erect over me and lowered yourself gently into my damp forest.

> We share a joint
> A glass of red
> I see your face
> Sebastian

Christ. Another waste of fucking time. *Ruth Life Map?* What the fuck was that? What I had to do was make *amends*, not write stupid lists. Phone Martin and apologise, stop buying drugs, get a new flat, get out of the Tracey situation without damaging her psyche too much (stop thinking it *would* damage her psyche), concentrate on work, sort out my future. Fall in love (either sex). How hard could it be? I had a line of coke and went into the kitchen. I might as well be nice to James as well – seeing I wouldn't be living with the filthy faggot for much longer. He was kneeling on all fours, up to his waist in underpants and the kitchen cupboards, pulling out rusty cheese graters and greasy peanut butter jars.

"James."

"Yes?" He bashed his head backing out of the cupboard. "It's *very* dirty in there Ruth. When was the last time it was cleaned?" he demanded.

"What are you doing?"

"I'm cleaning the kitchen cupboards."

"You've never cleaned anything in here before, why are you doing it now? And why don't you put some fucking trousers on?"

"I'm doing my share of the housework," he said haughtily and clambered back under the sink, Y-fronts stretching across the highways and byways of his well-travelled backside.

"Are you going to work today?" I said.

"Yes."

"Good."

I was glad. If James was at home on a Saturday it'd be gayboy station by lunchtime: they started gathering at about eleven and the lounge would be full of them by mid-afternoon, by which time they'd be bored and have to go out for coffee, coming back early evening to mill about and watch TV and make phone calls before returning to their respective lairs to iron shirts and take drugs.

I left him to it and went into the lounge to call Martin. I didn't have the energy to resolve anything with James – he was on his own trip – but I couldn't leave things the way they were with Martin. And what about Tracey?

Give the girl a chance. Christ.

I could hear my mother saying it, even though I knew it couldn't be my mother. My mother would have thought we were both perverts. *What the bloody hell do you think you're playing at?... Well?*

I went down the hall and opened the front door to let some air in. It had started to rain. I stood there looking out at the world. Rain landed on the doormat which was coming undone at one end. I knew how it felt.

What was it with me?

Nothing changed.

I stood there watching the rain, thinking about when I was a kid and went to the fair with my parents. I was only about four. I got a toy gun in the lucky dip, one that fired plastic arrows with suction caps on the end. It was a boy's prize. I didn't want a boy's one. I wanted a girl's one. *No! I don't want it.*

I carried it anyway. Tightly under one arm as we walked down the bright street back to the car. And when we got there, I went to look at it… and I'd dropped it. My father walked the entire length of the street but it was gone. Someone else had got it. I went home empty-handed.

I often thought about it: it was a recurring glimpse of my childhood. The absolute devastation I felt upon losing that gun.

I rang Tracey's house to leave a message for her. *Sarah speaking.* I could hear laughter in the background and then Tracey came to the phone.

"How's the cat?"

"Why are you ringing me?"

"I was going to leave a message. I didn't think you'd be there. What are you doing?"

"Nothing."

"Where's Alicia? Did you have a fight?"

"Yeah… Sorry I hung up."

"That's all right. Do you want to come over here?"

"I haven't got a car –" she said hopefully.

"Don't worry. I'll come and pick you up. Is Alicia still there?"

"No. They went out."

"OK, I'll pick you up this afternoon. Come over for dinner if you like."

We said our goodbyes and as I put the phone down it rang again.

"Good, I'm glad I've caught you. It's Muriel."

Muriel was one of Liz's showbiz cronies who wrote a newspaper column and spelt everyone's name wrong. She was low-life, slightly dumb. Dangerous as fuck to anybody newsworthy.

"I'm having a dinner tonight for Malcolm Bates, and Elspeth Das cancelled and I was casting around for someone interesting – and I thought of you!"

Interesting. I was flattered.

"Malcolm Bates?" I said, wanting to see how far Muriel would go in trying to make me.

"You haven't got any plans have you?"

"I have actually, Muriel. A friend's coming round for dinner."

"You'll have to cancel it."

I laughed. "I can't do that."

"Man or woman?"

"Woman –"

"Good. Bring her with you. Is she good-looking?"

"She is, but –"

"Even better," she said. "Now, wear something dressy and tell your friend to. What's your friend's name?"

I went for black and was just wondering if I looked all right when the taxi pulled up outside. Tracey was in the back. She waved. I had a last puff on a joint and sprayed perfume around and ran outside. Tracey was wearing a long black dress and an oversized jacket over the top of it.

"Hi," I said, climbing in.

"Hi." She moved along the seat. "You smell nice."

"Thanks. So do you. What are you wearing?" I opened her jacket.

"Is this all right?" she said.

"Yeah. You can take the jacket off when we get there."

"No, I don't want to."

"Why not?"

She indicated her breasts.

"Don't be silly," I said. "You look great."

She looked out the window.

"You do. Honestly."

"Thanks." She turned and smiled at me and moved closer, reaching for my hand. We both saw the driver looking at us in the mirror and laughed. I held her hand. She'd painted her nails green and had a green bracelet on.

"Have you met Malcolm Bates before?" she said. "I can't believe I'm going to meet him. He's amazing. I saw him in a play once. Who else is going to be there?"

I laughed. "Don't get too excited."

"Thanks for ringing me back."

"That's all right. I was meaning to ask you –"

"What?" she squeezed my hand. Best friends.

"I just wondered why you were on Prozac?"

"I told you. Depression."

"Have you been taking it for a while?"

"Yeah. Have one," she said and laughed, reaching for her bag.

Muriel lived by herself in a three-bedroom house which she was renovating. Her latest triumph was a kitchen bar. Everything was spotless and in working order; pale walls and ruched drapes. She was delighted with Tracey. She laughed when she opened the door and saw her. Tracey was all over her from the second we arrived: there were kisses and hugs and then Muriel was showing Tracey the new rug and trying to stop her dog Missy from pissing on us or whatever it was trying to do and pointing out where the ceiling lights had been before she had the new lighting plan installed. I was exhausted by the time we reached the kitchen.

"Good. Now I'm glad you didn't bring anything to drink. We're drinking gin. Missy. Get down. Rebecca and Adrian, this is Ruth and Tracey. Malcolm's not here yet. What do you think of the kitchen bar?"

"It's amazing," Tracey said. "Hi Rebecca!"

Rebecca looked pleased and shook hands. She was pretty. Young with brown hair and brown lipstick. Expensive dress. Adrian, a kind of

Mediterranean ingenue, except he was a man and about forty, breathed in, and shook Tracey's hand softly. When it was my turn he held my hand in both of his and said *Ruth*. I wasn't sure what I was supposed to say. Yes I *do* want to suck your cock Adrian. *Soon.*

"Rebecca's a makeup artist, and Adrian is – what are you Adrian?" Muriel said from behind the kitchen bar.

"In love," he said, looking at Tracey.

Everyone laughed.

Tracey took her jacket off. She was wearing a black sleeveless evening dress and looked ten feet tall. One of the seams was coming apart at the back. Adrian watched her undress and then slid into the kitchen area to look over Muriel's shoulder while she poured the gin. Missy was sniffing at the hem of Tracey's dress.

"Hello darling!" Tracey said. "Up you come."

Missy licked Tracey's neck, happily ensconced.

"Come through to the front room," Muriel said, handing us our drinks. "I've got the fire going. I *love* your dress," she said to Tracey.

"Thank you," Tracey said, following her. "Thanks for inviting me."

We were all grouped around the fireplace commenting on the drapes when the doorbell rang. Muriel went to answer it and came back with Malcolm Bates. He was dressed in jeans and old boat shoes, with a paunch. He looked at us disparagingly and scratched his head before following Muriel to the kitchen to get a drink.

"He's always like that," Rebecca confided in us. "He's really talented."

Tracey was fizzing with excitement. She could barely contain herself. She looked at the door and grinned at me and then thought about something and then inadvertently struck a gay young thing pose, one hand holding the edge of the mantelpiece and the other holding Missy. She realised what she was doing and quickly looked in her underarm area and straightened up, glancing at me and batting Missy on the head. Rebecca started talking to me and I watched Adrian move in on Tracey. Malcolm Bates came back into the room, averting his eyes and sitting on the couch with his drink. He picked up a magazine and looked at the cover of it.

"Righto everyone," Muriel said, coming in and turning the music down. "This is Malcolm," she said, "Malcolm, come and say hello to everyone."

It was like a press launch. Malcolm got up reluctantly and said hello and then sat down again with his magazine. Muriel turned the music up and made a big fuss of a new arrival, a stocky young man called Simon who wanted a beer.

"I'll get it," I said.

The doorbell rang as I was going down the hall. An auburn-haired woman was on the doorstep in a low-cut dress and a shawl. She smiled. She had beautiful deep sea eyes.

"Hello," I said. "They're all in there."

I showed her to the lounge and hurried to the kitchen to get the beer so I could get back and find out who she was.

Her name was Natalie. She was the leading lady in Malcolm Bates's new movie. She sat next to him on the couch and they talked earnestly; Muriel was talking to Simon and frowning slightly as she tried to concentrate on two conversations at once. I stood at the fire-place for a while and then (mysteriously) went to the kitchen to top up my gin. I didn't mind being by myself: they all got round to you eventually.

The table had been set in the dining room and a smaller table had been added to one end, with one place setting on it. Tracey.

When I got back Tracey was sitting on the couch listening to Natalie attentively. Malcolm Bates saw me looking and his eyes flew off to another branch.

I took a big swallow of my gin. I was getting drunk. Muriel came over and asked if Liz was having a good holiday and then said quietly to my collarbone, "They're getting on well," meaning Natalie and Tracey.

"Who are?" I said looking over at them.

"Aw," she cawed, quick as a wink, "wouldn't it be luv-erly," and then laughed at herself. "Lucky old Liz. Now. *Food.* I hope you like sushi, Malcolm. You come with me Missy."

Missy jumped down and Natalie and Tracey watched her scamper out the door and then smiled at each other. Tracey looked guiltily at me and excused herself.

"She's an actress," she said. She pulled at her knickers beneath her dress. "Come on, let's get a seat."

"In a minute. I just want some of this." I'd been watching Adrian take a joint out of his pocket and light it up. He had a puff and passed it to Tracey who flicked her hair and took it carefully between her fingers. "Thank you," she said.

"And how do you occupy your time, Tracey?" Adrian asked.

"Me?" She laughed. "Media studies. I'm doing a degree." She took another puff and went to hand it back to him.

"*I want some,*" I said, reaching for it.

"Sorry." Tracey laughed again, looking to see if Malcolm had seen her.

What a star fuck. She was beginning to piss me off.

She brushed her hair off her face and then hooked one arm through Adrian's and announced, "Adrian's coming to dinner with me!"

Adrian laughed, giving her an appraising look before allowing her to lead him through the door. They were followed by Natalie and Malcolm Bates and then Rebecca and Simon. I was left standing at the fireplace holding the joint, mildly worried about the seating arrangements. Shit. I'd have to go in by myself now. I rushed down the empty hall and then slowed up when I reached the dining room and casually entered.

They were all seated in their adult chairs, touching cutlery and adjusting clothing. Tracey gave me a sympathetic look – from between Natalie and Adrian.

"Am I – ?"

"Yes. That's you," Muriel smiled at me from the head of the table.

I sat down, but it was a longer drop than I thought and I nearly pulled the tablecloth off as I tried to get my legs under the annexe. Simon was on one side and Rebecca on the other, both considerably higher than me.

Simon coughed and filled up his glass.

"Would you like some?" he asked me.

"Thanks."

"How's work, Rebecca?" he said.

"Wonderful!" she said, and they pulled out of the station, on board the conversation train, leaving me to my annexe. Nobody looked at me. Muriel lit the candles and turned the music up, and they all started talking loudly. Even Malcolm Bates, who was now assured of his position as most important guest at the dinner party. And I was the *least* important person there. And nobody was talking to me! Fucking Tracey. She was revelling in it. Adrian was quietly licking her face and Malcolm Bates was lining up for a lick as she effortlessly beguiled the two of them, attempting to hook in Natalie along the way.

I kept up a good facade though. Smiling and listening to Rebecca and Simon until they felt obliged to include me, which resulted in a dull tale about Simon's driving job before they got back into the saddle and cantered off down Enjoying Themselves Street again.

I was drunk. I started to focus on the ridge between the two tables, wondering what the table was like underneath, not the big table – my little table. Where Muriel had got it from. Maybe she got it from the shed and it still had dirt on it. Or cobwebs.

"Is that your natural hair colour?" Rebecca asked.

I wanted to leap out of my chair and spring into her lap and sit there, looking down at my cage, wagging my tail.

Muriel served up the first course.

"I feel like I'm about six in this chair," I laughed as she got to me.

"Do you?" she said. "You don't look it dear," and I heard Tracey's guffaw cut through the rest.

The *fucking* bitch.

I take her out to someone *I* know (to be *kind* to her) and she nabs the best seat and does her Miss Popularity impression and then she fucking *laughs* at me. I glared at her, not caring who saw.

"Don't be so grumpy," she said, "*I'll* sit there."

"*No*," I said, but she was already on her way down. Adrian was laughing and Malcolm Bates was looking curiously at me.

"Come on," she said, shaking the back of my chair. "Get up."

"Piss off," I said.

"How *rude*." She laughed again and Adrian wiped the still-warm spittle from the cleft of his chin.

I got up and slunk to the front.

"Hi," I said, sitting down, feeling the heat of Tracey's bottom.

"I love this seat," Tracey said. "It's so *cute*."

And indeed she did look cute in it. Glorious. Splendid. More pretty than pretty has a right to be.

And now it was Tracey's party and we were all in the wrong size chairs.

"Your turn Natalie!" Tracey had found a board game on Muriel's bookshelf and persuaded Muriel to let us play it. She handed out pads and pencils and made everyone shut up while she read out the instructions. I made subversive comments and drew a picture of a woman with large breasts before going to the lounge, much to Muriel, Tracey and Adrian's relief. Simon was making going-home noises and didn't care what I was up to, and Malcolm Bates and Rebecca were slurring over each other in the darkest corner of the table. Natalie looked like she might have wanted me to stay, but I knew I wouldn't have a shit show in hell of getting the ropes undone without Tracey noticing.

It was one o'clock in the morning. I was sitting outside in a plastic chair, covered in dog hair. Tracey was still conducting proceedings indoors: seeing Adrian off (Adri-*an!* Stop it!); helping Muriel load the dishwasher (Shall I put these in here?); chatting about how brilliant it was to meet Malcolm Bates (Where do you think they *went* to?!) and how amazing Natalie was.

I was spinning out. I tried to stand up and dropped my glass on the patio. Tracey came running out. Cinders till the end.

"Are you all right?" she said, picking up the broken glass.

"Yes thank you."

Seems a lot of people were asking me that question lately.

I made it to standing position and lurched indoors, past Troll Muriel and out the front door to the car.

Next thing we're in bed and I'm suffocating between two flaps of bleeding cow's tongue. I can't get my nose out. *Help... Me!* I must have buckled in panic; her thighs unlocked and she lifted herself off me. Like a shipwrecked sailor finding shore I breathed once and passed out: my head swirling with a queasy cocktail of gin and cunt smells.

8: Flurries of minor violence

Madamski left in a huff first thing in the morning after I made some alleged comment about her belle of the ball routine and then vomited gin and sushi into the kitchen sink. After she'd gone I put a raincoat on and marched down the road to buy some juice, standing dry-mouthed and confused in front of the drinks cabinet.

I couldn't leave things the way they were with Martin. But I had to work out what to say to him first... What could I say? I decided to ring him. But I didn't really want to speak to him. Perhaps his answerphone would be on and I could just leave a message. Or I could just forget about it and not bother. But I really liked him. I might even be in love with him. I blatted home and stood in the lounge in front of the telephone, my hands sweating and my heart skipping prettily every time I went to pick up the phone.

I might even be in love with him?

I'd been in love a few times. Once with Mark Legat, an overbearing estate agent with bulk money and anal warts. He was a classic psycho, sneaking around the house like an Alsatian checking to see if I'd been anywhere near his clothes, which he kept in small piles on top of cardboard boxes half-full of receipts and coat hangers and ironed tea towels. He used to get annoyed if I touched anything that belonged to him. He never let me anywhere near the kitchen either, groaning if I so much as picked up the dishcloth, and grabbing it off me to swipe at the kitchen bench yet again.

He did all the cooking: roasts were his speciality, anything meaty... gigantic steaks submerged in red wine and blood, lamb chops basted lovingly for hours with honey and mint, anything like that. We must have had vegetables but I can't remember having them; if we did they would have been roasted, or fried, or something that involved the oven, or fat. I think we had salads occasionally; I know he liked spring onions and roast beef sandwiches.

He was always very cagey about the warts and eventually had them burnt off in a private clinic. A few weeks later I was looking through a medical dictionary and discovered that anal warts only come from anal sex. It sort of fell apart after that... every time I looked at his head it reminded me of a huge penis: like an engorged talking penis jiggling around between his shoulders. I told him this one night when we were drunk at a restaurant and he was almost sick with disgust. He stopped eating and threw down his serviette, which he had tucked down the front of his shirt, and then lit a cigarette and squinted disdainfully through the smoke at me.

I still don't know what he saw in me, although he used to bray to his builder friends that I liked sleeping with women, and he was forever trying to convince female estate agents into coming home with us. He managed to persuade one or two of them as well, luring them in with speed and champagne, and me, I suppose: I remember I looked very innocent at the time – I was going through an ankle-bracelet phase and never bothered to brush my hair. After we broke up I didn't see him for years, and then I bumped into him one night at a party. He was fat, and still stewing in Van Cleef & Arpels.

I'd been childishly in love with Vicki Honey. She rode a Kawasaki 125 and looked like Elvis Presley. I followed her around for months until she finally gave in and kissed me spectacularly in the pub toilets one night. To my eternal shame I covered a notebook in crushed blue velvet and wrote all my favourite poems in it and presented it to her, and when she decided she wasn't gay I parked at the end of her street and watched her come and go, my world crashing around me when she arrived home one evening with a bearded pillion passenger. I sat there for five hours until her bedroom light finally went out at 2am. I was there again at eight the next morning and watched them put their helmets on and fool around on the footpath, slapping each other's leather jackets affectionately.

I'd had other brushes with love, the usual heart-stopping moments amongst them, the days and days in bed, the tranquillity and discovery, the mind and body opiated, satiated: you simply don't care what anyone else is doing, lock the door, leave us be. I like being in love, who doesn't?... in the beginning. But it always turns to crap. You waltz blindly down the road towards indifference, or distaste: flurries of minor violence, a drunken chest pummelling session, or the odd shoulder push signalling the way.

But I wasn't going to worry about that at the moment. I picked up the phone and dialled his number. His *special* number (for now it was).

"Hello Martin? It's Ruth."

"Hello."

"I'm just ringing to see if you got your coat..."

Nothing.

"Are you there?"

"Yep."

"I'm sorry about the other night."

"Who did you end up sleeping with?"

"What?"

"Did you sleep with Sebastian?"

"No, don't be stupid." I forced a laugh. "How did the ad come out?"

"Good."

"What made you think I slept with Sebastian?"

"Don't you remember?"

What?

Shit.

"That's why I wanted to ring you," I said. "I, I'm –"

"You're what?" he said.

"I'm really embarrassed."

(*What about? What about? What about?*)

"Mm."

Doomed.

"Well, anyway, I just rang to apologise –"

"Maybe you should apologise to Lorna."

Lorna?

"OK."

More silence.

"Shall I come over and see you?" I said, "I could bring something with me. A few things actually. I'll come over and see you this afternoon. About three, OK?"

He hesitated so I said *see you then* and hung up before he could say no.

I had another chance. Thank God, thank God. But... what did he mean when he said *Don't you remember?*

9: Nirvana

Best to forget it. I had another chance, that was the main thing. What to wear? At the back of my diary, in the December pages, I sometimes jotted down combinations of clothes that worked well on the day, in case I needed inspiration in a hurry, but whenever I looked at them again I'd invariably be taken aback by my own bad taste. A *beret?*

Maybe I'd go for the Laura Ashley look: Ruth the innocent gathers the morning's eggs from the chicken coop, *Good morning chickens! It's Ruuuth!* Or something more urban? Something baggy, or Nepalese striped? Schoolgirl? I had some over-the-knee socks somewhere...

It was at this point that I should have hoved to, gone below to read the chart, instead of cracking on ahead like an enthusiastic fool, recklessly ignoring all the other shit that was going on. Of course, now I can see how ridiculous I was, how lacking in perceptivity about myself and others, but I couldn't have seen it then – even if I'd been dragged aside and had my nose rubbed in it. I was on auto-pilot, even though I was totally without direction.

I feel like two people in that respect, that I can't possibly be the person I'm writing about, but I am, *I am*: a small nightmare in the history of humankind.

Dee and Ray came around earlier today and had a cup of coffee. Dee saw the word processor and asked what I was writing. *I hope I'm in it*, she said, and when I told her she was, she demanded to read it, and I said she couldn't because it wasn't finished, so she tussled with me over the kitchen table and stalked off into the garden with a few pages from the second chapter, which she isn't in. Ray went out and took them off her before she had a chance to read them, and she followed him in and sneered at me, *You think you're clever don't you?* and sat on the couch with her legs apart, deliberately obscene.

"Come on Dee," Ray said. "That's not fair."

"What the fuck would you know about fair?" she said. "You wouldn't fugging know."

It was only then that I realised how out of it she was. Ray offered to make the coffee, dithering around in the kitchen while Dee slumped on the couch nodding off, her surprisingly soft-looking cunt making an appearance every so often. Ray didn't ask where the cups were, or the sugar: he improvised if he got stuck; I wanted to hug him for it. It occurred to me that I'd always been attracted to the Dees and the Rays, and even the Traceys I suppose. And it patently wasn't a case of opposites attracting: I was right in there with them, gobbling my Valium, no future to speak of, only a past I'd rather forget.

I went for a black polo neck and an old leather jacket: the accomplished director look. I nearly got carried away and hung a stopwatch around my neck for effect... And *cut*. Good, that was good that time everyone. Thank you. Let's set up for the next shot please. (Modest throat clearing.) Lunch? Yes, *lunch*, why not?... What's that darling?... No, no, you were good Nastassja. *Yes, really*.

Sebastian phoned while I was getting ready. I told him I was going round to Martin's which shut him up: he'd rung to ask if I wanted to go out for a drive and afternoon tea. Judging from our last tryst, one would have assumed there was more likelihood of me being up for sex on all fours, followed by a nude swim. Afternoon tea in his fucking Rover? I made it sound like Martin was my boyfriend and there was something unresolved between us. I left awkward pauses where my bits should have been and said *Sorry Sebastian, I hope you didn't think...* and trailed off apologetically, and he really loved me by the end of it: I could hear the undisguised regret in his voice as he said goodbye and waited for me to hang up. I felt a pang of remorse, but nothing major. After I got off the phone I checked my lipstick in the mirror. I'd tried brown, but it looked awful so I went to the bathroom to get some toilet paper to wipe it off with. The toilet bowl had some-thing in it; I didn't want to look but it was hard to avoid, and when I did look I felt *affronted*: it's a shit as round as a mug of tea; it looks like an elephant's done it. A wet rag of toilet paper had been dropped carelessly on one end of it… It was so big I thought I'd give James the benefit of the doubt, but when I flushed the toilet it slipped away without any trouble whatsoever. What was really weird was that I walked into James on my way out of the bathroom: he was leaning against the door as if he'd been standing there for a while. He was still wearing the day before's underpants and for a moment I thought he might whip his dick out and come running down the hall after me… *I'm going to get yooooo…*

I left without saying goodbye to the invert. The afternoon seemed full of possibility: I felt like I'd just come from the international air-port, frisky with sophistication and about to be reunited with my lover who would be earnestly writing me a thirty-page letter with lit-tle kisses all through it and mid-sentence I LOVE YOUs (exclamation mark, exclamation mark).

The bit from the car to Martin's door even went well; I looked in at the man in the cycle shop and checked out a few bike prices before pressing Martin's buzzer.

There was an empty beer can in his doorway so I picked it up. Rubbish frightened me. The fucking *amount* of it. My parents didn't recycle anything: they resented someone else making money while they had to do all the work – sorting out the green bottles from the brown, working out which slot to put the cans in. *Why should some other bastard make money out of us?* my mother would say, watching my father wheeling huge piles of crap to the gate for the rubbish truck to collect, *you must think we're stupid*, and she'd look at me suspi-ciously, suspecting that I did. She thought I was a zealot, a weirdo: she'd look at me the same way the girl at the chemist shop did when I said, *No don't worry, I don't need another bag.* You could see their minds ticking over, trying to work out *Why*.

Martin answered the door and I handed him the can.

"It was there," I said, and pointed to the ground. "Have you got a bin?"

"Yeah." We went upstairs and he took the can into the kitchen. I couldn't look at him when he came back, preferring to study a pamphlet on film stock which I found on the couch.

He stood in front of me and said hesitantly, "Ah, yeah –"

"What?" I said, looking at his dirty feet. Whatever he was about to say I didn't think I was going to like it. I reached for my bag, the old standby. "Do you want a line?"

"Yeah?" he lightened up. "Do you want a beer?"

There was an air of reprieve in the room as I set about chopping out the coke and he went to get the beer. There were some flowers in a vase on the shelf with a big blue bow tied round the stems. He came in with the beer and sat opposite me.

"Thanks." I smiled stiffly at him, looking at him properly for the first time since I'd arrived. His hands shook slightly as he lit a cigarette. He smoked cigarettes in a way that made you want to take it up yourself, and when he smoked, from certain angles he looked like a woman.

"I'll try not to rip up your magazines this time."

"Yeah," he said eagerly, and laughed. "The guy didn't want it back anyway."

There was something strange going on here. Why was *he* nervous?

He had his coke and then sniffed and bared his teeth. "Excellent. Thanks."

I snorted my line with as much grace as I could muster, wondering if he was looking at the blackheads on my nose, then sat back, trying to look relaxed.

"They're nice flowers," I said.

"Yeah," he said, not looking at them.

"I'm really sorry about the other night…"

"Yeah?" He looked directly at me which caused multiple eruptions in my chest and great molten lava flows began to spew steadily out of me on to the floor.

"Mmm," he said slowly, still watching me, his eyes smiling. The look was pure sex. It said fuck me, fuck me now.

FUCK ME.

My entire body was expanding: I had that peculiar light throbbing starting up between my legs and my breasts felt like they were filling up with liquid, on slow fill, amplified with lust.

"Are you OK?" I asked pointlessly and had a mouthful of beer, not taking my eyes off him.

"I'm fine," he said, smiling, and got up. "Come into the bedroom if you like."

I followed him to his bedroom and he shut the door quietly behind me and kissed me. I felt like I was going to faint. He brushed his hand gently between my legs, then pulled me down onto the bed. A newspaper fluttered to the floor like confetti.

"Do you want to take your clothes off?" he asked.

I said something. I don't know what. I didn't know what I was saying. I could have been saying anything.

"Take this off." He pulled at my jacket.

I got undressed with my back to him and jumped into bed where he was already waiting, felt the unfamiliar flesh against mine, then his hands all over me, then... you don't care. He opened my legs and pushed into me; I was swooning, staring, I was bodysurfing in summer, waves deep green and clean... up... and... o

He came, shuddering into me, then lay there for a moment before slipping out.

"Sorry," he said.

"That's OK."

"I don't have AIDS."

"That's OK, neither do I."

I lay there feeling stupid and then smiled at him and reached for his hand and placed it on my stomach. He looked amused and got out of bed and put his trousers on.

"All right?" he said.

"Good. Thanks." I covered myself with the duvet and reached out to touch his back as he walked away, but missed, and my hand flopped over the side of the bed. I could hear him mucking around in the lounge and then coming back down the hall. He came in with the beer and handed me one, before picking up the paper and sitting in the chair by the bed, reading.

"I thought you were gay," I grinned.

He looked up from the paper. "Do you think I am now?"

"I don't know. You might be," I smiled.

There was an awful lot of smiling going on (me). Grinning, smirking, beaming... general goofing off, post-coital backslapping, inner-sanctum celebrating – Ah, we've had some news guys, your single's just gone to No. 1 in the charts. Right, can I get anyone a beer, or shall we crack open the champagne? I think so, I fucking *think so,* order some fucking champagne! I can't *fucking believe* it! Wooh! We Fucking Did It! *You* Fucking Did It! No, no, don't answer the phone, we've gotta think about this, we gotta work out what we're gonna do, *cool, cool...*

(One minute you're lugging the PA around for some band who've got a five-album record deal (the cunts), plugging in their mics and thinking about blowing your brains out, self-consciously handing your demo tape to their manager; and the next you're on stage doing the support tour, rapidly shrugging off your new-boy status, taking to it like a duck to water, pissed off that it took so long. Those cunts. Those fucking record company cunts.)

Yes sir, I WAS THAT ROCK STAR.

I WAS IN LOVE.

I took a deep breath and had a mouthful of beer. It was silent in the room except for the occasional turning of the page. I looked around the room. There wasn't much in it: the bed with one pillow and no cover on the duvet, the chair he was sitting in, several pairs of shoes, a digital clock, a pen, and a glass of water with dust and a pubic hair floating on top of it... that was about it.

I leaned over and pinched the hair out of the glass and, checking to make sure he wasn't watching, had a quick look at it.

It didn't look like one of mine. Mine were longer.

He belched and looked up from the paper. "What are you doing today?"

"Pardon?"

"Have you got anything planned?"

"No. Why, have you?"

"Yeah, yeah I have, I've got to go and see somebody, in about half an hour."

He was lying: I recognised the pitch, the intonation, the fucking *reason*.

"Oh." I had another swig of beer. "I brought you a trip."

"Excellent," he said, balancing on the back legs of the chair and lifting the Venetian blind to look outside, "I feel like having a trip."

"I'll go and get it," I said. "You don't have a – ?" I was going to ask for a dressing gown, but instead I pulled back the sheet and lay there provocatively, pole dancer pleases western businessman. *My famiry very por.*

"What kind of trips are they?" he said.

"What?"

He shook the paper. "What kind of trips are they?"

God. I pulled the sheet up and rolled over to the opposite side of the bed, the tips of my fingers stinging with the effort it took to get the sheet to come with me. Blushing like a bowl of strawberries I sat up with my back to him, rubbing my face. "I'm not sure, I got them off someone at work."

"I've got to make a phone call." He put his shirt on and left the room.

I sat there for a while and then went over to the window. In the street below a woman was leading a little boy around, showing him this and that. He stopped to pick up something and the woman talked him through it. You could believe anything when you were two years old: if a six-headed alien ambled up to you and said hello and your mother didn't flinch, you'd be smiling at it in a few minutes. That *alien* mummy. The whole thing was just one big mind fuck. Here I was in Martin Myers's bedroom, and for all intents and purposes I'd got what I wanted: I'd connected with him in some way – albeit briefly. Very briefly, come to think of it. The whole thing had only lasted about a minute and a half. Maybe he just wanted a fuck, I had no idea. I knew I found everything about him compelling. Everything. The way he looked, the way his hair smelt a bit like a cat's, the clothes he wore... Every fucking thing. His pubic hair. Those shoes. That pen.

I could hear him in the lounge on the phone to somebody. They were talking about hiring an underwater camera. I got dressed, spending two minutes frantically searching for my knickers which I eventually found tangled up in the sheet. He was in the kitchen making a cup of coffee. I snuck a look at him; his jaw was twitching.

"How's the coke?" I asked.

"Excellent." He poured the boiling water into the cups, letting the spoon clatter onto the bench. "What's the time?"

I knew he really wanted to say, "Where's the acid?" but he was waiting for me to bring the subject up.

"I'm not sure. Do you want that trip now?"

"Yeah, great. Sugar?"

Oh honey honey. You are my candy giiiiiirl, and you got me wanting you.

"Okey pokey," I said, and started to blush again. *Okey pokey?* "I'll get my bag."

I went into the lounge and sneaked over to the flowers to read the card. *Fiona, thanks for all your help. Love Jill.* Who was Fiona? Who was Jill for that matter? And why were her flowers on his shelf? He must have a girlfriend. But she'd never been here when I'd been here, and he'd never mentioned her. But why would he? Why should he? I went back to the kitchen, determined not to say anything about it.

"Who's Fiona?" I said, picking up my coffee, my heart stopping at the top of the Ferris wheel.

"Who?"

"The flowers –"

"She's my producer. Did you get the acid?"

"Oh. Sorry. I forgot." I went back to the lounge and found my bag, swinging it to and fro as I walked into the kitchen, trying to pretend I belonged there now that I'd earned my Quick Fuck badge.

I gave Martin half a trip and he put it in his mouth.

"Have the other half," I said.

"Is it strong?"

"No, not really." I put two halves on my own tongue, a hard little chemical taste mixing with saliva as I chewed it to a pulp and then washed it down with coffee. He put the milk back in the fridge and I followed him as far as the bench and stood there watching him. He came over to the bench to get his coffee and I moved clumsily over to the fridge and picked up a fridge magnet.

"This is nice," I said. It was a fucking *hamburger*.

He looked at me out of the corner of his eye as he surveyed the road below.

"So, what's happening then?" he said.

"What?"

"What are you up to now?" he asked, taking noisy gulps of his coffee.

"I'm not sure. Why, what are you doing?"

"I've got to organise some things for a shoot," he said, looking directly at me.

"Do you need any help?"

"No, it's all sorted. Thanks." He brushed some sugar off the bench. "What?"

"Is that it then?"

"What?"

"Forget it. I'll see you later." I grabbed my bag and walked out the door.

"Hey," he called half-heartedly after me. "Where are you going?"

"Home." I ran down the stairs and back to the car. Fucking worm. No wonder he was so fucking polite. Shit. Shit shit shit. My chest tightened and I started the car and put it into first, fussing about in the glovebox moving maps and cassettes around, stalling in case he was going to come after me. No sign of him.

Fuck him. I didn't need him. I drove off angrily.

It was at that moment, just as I was accelerating away, crashing into second, that I realised with something relatively close to terror that I'd just chewed my way through one large portion of LSD.

Or whatever the fuck it was.

10: Hiya Ruthy

"So you believe this... *trip*... was instrumental in... triggering some form of... mental illness?"

That's correct Hilary. And the rest.

Hilary Hancock waited patiently for my answer; beige dress splayed over wide hips; lumpy legs crossed at the ankles. We were sitting opposite each other on small two-seater couches in her small two-seater office.

I knew the instant I saw her that I'd fucked up: she came shunting out of her office and our eyes locked for a mutually disappointing moment before I trailed in after her, hoping I wouldn't have to lie down anywhere. I thought she'd taken me to the wrong room – or we were going to have a cup of tea or something – but she gestured for me to sit down and then sat down herself with a rich underskirt waft that reminded me of my mother (sitting on the toilet in front of me, farting, or wiping blood from between her legs, while I stood there, shocked at her lack of concern, not wanting to bear witness to that bushy place), and said pleasantly, *And how can I help you Ruth?*

Er...?

Where would you like me to start?

We'd done parents (Q: Did you *like* your mother? A: No, not particularly. Q: What about your father, what was your... relationship with him? A: I don't know. Not very good); childhood generally (Q: Would you say you had a... *happy* childhood? A: No); with an edited version of the whys and wherefores, and now we were up to ye olde trippe.

"Do you want to talk about it?" she asked, and recrossed her ankles.

"Not really. I don't remember that much about it," I lied.

"No," she agreed, "and, and..." she groped around momentarily, "you think that, ah... *Michael* was using you?"

"Martin."

"Martin," she said, doing a little half-nod thing with her head and thinking deeply for a moment. "Is there any reason *why* you think he was doing this?"

"Ah... he wanted a *fuck?*" I said under my breath, looking at her brown criss-crossy sandals. I was going to apologise, but changed my mind when I saw her blinking faster and looking towards the door.

"She can't help you now," I said.

"What?" She looked startled.

"Nothing. Actually, I've got to get going –"

"Oh –" she said, surprised, "we've only just sta–"

I stood up. "Shall I pay the receptionist?"

"Yes. Yes. If you don't mind. I'm glad I –"

Oh fuck off.

She followed me out and ruffled through some files while I paid the bill.

I wanted to refuse to pay but I didn't have the courage. Pull out a pistol and wave it round in the air and fire a couple of rounds at her ankles. Run out of the building screaming.

"Thank you," I said. "Thanks very much."

I went outside to wait for Ray who was picking me up. It was his fucking fault I was there. He'd been round earlier in the week, by himself – apparently Dee was on some sort of bender and didn't want to see me because I was writing a book. I told Ray it wasn't a book per se, it was just a few thoughts, more like an autobiography sort of thing (trying to play it down). Anyway, she's a bit fucked up by it all: it's brought up the past and her own book... *I think its success is sporadic... in the end I'm sorry to say I don't want to make an offer.* My fucking fault again. Fucking hell, whatever happened to peace love and fucking happiness? I felt like going on a fucking bender myself, but Ray seemed like such a poor companion, and there's no one else to ring, so I didn't.

While he was making the coffee Ray had mentioned he'd been to counselling once. I wasn't sure what he was getting at, he didn't seem to be saying I should go to counselling, just that he'd been. I thought about it after he'd gone: counselling sounded a bit wishy-washy so I went for the top shelf and looked up psychiatrists in the Yellow Pages. They were under psychotherapists. So I was now officially *in therapy.* What a fucking waste of money. Maybe I should have bored the crap out of odoriferous pants and told her about the trip. All fourteen hours of it...

"*James!*"

"Hi-eeee."

"*Where are you?*"

"In my bedroom."

I ran in. He was in bed with a small hairy thing.

"Fuck. Shit," I said.

"Hi-eeee," he said, propping himself up on one elbow.

"What's that?" I pointed at it rudely.

"Mario. He likes girls, don't you Mario? Hop in."

I ran into the lounge and perched on the edge of the couch staring wildly at the carpet. Everything was moving. The walls and the floor and the whole world was pulsating. It was all coming to life. It all *was alive* only I couldn't see it before. James came into the room naked, his dick bobbing about between his legs.

"*James.*"

He looked down and covered it with his hand, and then immediately forgot that that was what he was supposed to be doing, and reached for his pipe on the mantelpiece.

"I've had a trip, it's, it's – can you take me to the hospital?"

"What's that love?" he said. "*Really?* Is it good acid?" He rubbed his hands gleefully.

"I don't know. I just want it to stop."

"Relax. Go with the flow," he said, lighting his pipe. "Come back into the bedroom."

I followed him blindly. The bed was empty.

"Where's – ?"

"Why don't you get in?"

"*What?*" I said, and started chewing on my fingernails.

"He's got a lovely big cock."

"Shut *up*. What about that Valium you gave me, have you got any more?"

"Mario," he called, "Ruth's tripping."

Mario, who looked like a Mario this time, climbed on the bed. He wasn't James's usual type. This one was about forty and hairy. And he did have a big cock. Or a short thick one at any rate.

"Hi Ruth," he said, obviously proud of it.

"Hi." I looked at his hairy black chest, big waves of chemical hell starting to wash over me.

"How is it?" he asked, lighting a cigarette.

"It's really strong. Everything's moving."

"Great," he said and smiled, which made me feel marginally better.

The two of them lay there reclining on the pillows, stark naked. James had a silly expression on his face and he kept leaning forward and pushing my shoulder and screeching.

Fuck, fuck.

I had to do something before it got any worse; it'd started coming on in the car on the way home, and I hadn't helped the situation by panicking so badly, *but everything was moving now.* This was for real.

"What do you think I should do?" I looked to Mario for guidance.

"Enjoy it." He moved his hairy leg closer so that it touched mine.

"Enjoy it," James parroted, pushing me again.

They were both leering at me. I got off the bed and backed out of the room which was collapsing in on itself like a piano accordion. I decided to go for a walk.

Clear my head.

OK OK. I was the one in control. Not the drug. And it wasn't going to last forever. It would wear off eventually.

I wondered how Martin was. I hoped he was freaking out. No I didn't. I had to talk to him. I dialled his number. His answerphone was on.

"Martin?"

I waited to see if he would pick it up.

"Martin? Are you there?"

"Wow," I said and put the phone down.

I stood there staring at the phone then went and got my coat.

I walked.

It was pitch black outside, and still; my shadow kept me company, swooping past me in the lamp light. No moon. My boots hit the pavement rhythmically and my blood pumped in time with the world around me. Everything was alive, electrical.

I walked through the park, not afraid to be there, gliding between the great oak trees monolithic with memories; sweeping past ferns and tall grasses that reached out to stroke my coat; standing at the swings watching the steel chain vibrate – the iron and carbon reworked, reincarnated as twin braids straddling a slice of wood that still pulsed with the lifeblood of the parent tree.

I walked.

Through the graveyard: a cacophony of silence, no spirits here – all gone, gone to be with those who still lived; past the church, and out through the gate, tracing my steps back to the park. Back to the essence.

It seemed that every thing on earth had significant purpose, and I was intrinsically part of that; but for what purpose? My mind was travelling at the speed of light, sparking with bizarre visions, unfolding; I thought of things I hadn't thought of in years: religion, spirituality, karmic law – subjects I'd outlawed in my visible world.

And what of *my* essence? What lay at the core *of me?*

I was like that crazy fairground ride that chugged slowly around, increasing speed, faster and faster, until it pinned you helplessly against the side of the spinning orb, out of control, *weeeeeeeeeeeeeeeeeeeeee...* and when it finally started to slow, when the exhilarated punters caught their breath and looked down, they marvelled at the fact that there was nothing in the middle but a big hole.

There was no essence; there was only a void.

And I pitched head first into it.

I was under the trees staring at the motorway traffic. Big trucks grinding past. Lights ebbing and flowing in the night mist. Don't let them get you.

There was a brick wall and I was walking past it, galloping past it, running. I put my arm out, held my knuckles against the yellow brick (road) and kept running. For all the pain.

a huge huge head and a tiny distorted doll's body

The Earth sits like a luminous ball in space and a man flies around it (Jesus?) towing a big white sheet, and all the crap in the world is sucked up into it; all the shit; all the murderers; all the paedophiles; all the stinking pollution; all the plastic bags and all the soft drink bottles; every single car and every single truck and every single arsehole you ever met is sucked up into the sack, which is now as big as the earth itself. He flies off like Superman. But where to? Even he doesn't know.

would just get bigger and bigger until it *was* the universe and I was nothing

until it was the universe

There. In the shadows. Nicotined fingers casually scratching his arse. Wearing a tracksuit. A dog sits at his feet; eyes like black cherries; waiting.

Hiya Ruthy.

Martin opened the door and took me upstairs and wrapped my hand in a tea towel. There were some other people there. I lay on the floor beside the couch and he got me a blanket. Someone kept asking if I was all right. It seemed important not to move. I was safe as long as I was on the floor. I lay there blanking everything out, grinding my teeth, hoping that everything might return to normal if I just lay there blanking everything out

Dawn. Martin is sitting at the table writing something in a note-book. He stretches his legs and lights a cigarette. I look at his knees, desperate to reach out and touch them. He gets up and turns the TV on and lies on the couch. I crawl over and pull myself up beside him, and we stay there, saying nothing, watching TV with the sound down. My head is tucked in under his chin and my ear is positioned directly above his Adam's apple; I try to time my breathing to coincide with his. I want to climb inside him.

"God, you look terrible! What's happened to your hand?"

Maxine got out of her chair and put her arm around my shoulders. "Hey. Are you all right?"

"Not really," I said, trying not to cry in front of her. "Is Liz back?"

"Yeah but she's not coming in till lunchtime. What did you do to your hand? Come and sit down." She led me over to the reception couch. The door opened and Mace came in.

"Morning. How was your – ? Oh, ah…"

"Good." Maxine said. "Can you look after reception for a minute?"

"Reception?"

"Just for a second."

"What do I do?" He put his satchel down and looked at the telephone.

"*Mace.*"

"I'll be all right," I said.

"No, don't be silly," Maxine said. "We'll go to the toilets and then I'll make you a cup of tea."

She led me into the women's toilets and ran some hot water in the basin. I stood there, wiping away tears with my good hand and holding the other one out for her to look at. It was still wrapped in the tea towel.

I looked at myself in the mirror. My coat had mud all over it. I looked like I'd been plugged into a battery charger overnight.

"It's stuck to it," Maxine said, gingerly unwrapping the tea towel. "Here, soak it in the water."

I watched her as she bent over the basin: her hair had a rich copper sheen to it that caught the light; each strand was magnified as it snaked down the side of her face. My stomach gurgled.

"Ruth."

"Sorry."

"Does it hurt?"

I looked at my hand. I could see the tiny veins just beneath the skin, and the flesh on my knuckles was stiff with dirt and coagulated blood. I lowered my hand into the water.

"Ouch," Maxine said.

"Yeah," I pulled my hand out and looked at it. "Shit."

I felt dizzy. The colour of the basin matched my face. Jesus, what a mess.

"I saw Tracey yesterday," Maxine said brightly, in an effort to bring the whole thing back to Monday morningness. "She came over with her bass."

"Her bass?" I stared at the plughole.

"Yeah. She's going to play bass. In the band."

"Oh."

"Yeah." Her hand dropped from where it had been resting on my arm.

"I should go home," I said.

Maxine stood there for a moment looking confused. "What happened?"

"Nothing," I said, trying not to cry again. "Just tripping. Can you give Liz a message please?"

Now, I see everything from that time in vignette form. Little snatches, like a short film: as though my attention span didn't stretch to anything longer than about eight minutes. Twelve max.

I could hear Tracey in the lounge talking to James. Four o'clock. I must have slept. I tried to move my hand but it had seized up into a claw. I'd wrapped a piece of old sheet around it before going to bed and there were septic red and yellow puddles oozing out along the knuckle ridge. I hid the whole mess away under the duvet, and felt it begin to throb back into life. Tracey came in carrying some flowers.

"Oh dear. What have you been up to?"

"How did you know I was here?"

"Maxine rang me. What happened?" She tossed the flowers on the bed. "Move over," she said, and pulled back the covers. She sat on the edge of the bed taking off her boots.

"What are you doing?"

"What does it look like?"

I moved over to the other side of the bed and she got in and smacked the pillow, then arranged it behind her head. "Right, tell me what happened then. Do you like these flowers?"

"Are you and Maxine friends now?"

"What?" She looked puzzled. "Why?"

It wasn't worth getting into.

"I didn't know you played the bass."

"*Didn't* you? Shall I make you a cup of tea?"

"No, you don't have to –"

"I know. I want to."

"Why?"

"Because." She scrunched up her face and brought it close to mine, and said in a baby voice, "'*Cos*," then looked into my eyes and smiled.

I tried to smile back, without much success. She grabbed the flowers, cheerfully stuffing the head of a broken one back into the bunch, and said in her normal voice, as if she'd invented them, "I love these flowers."

"Really?" I said, unwilling to concede the patent.

"They're my favourite. Right, now you have a rest. I'll bring you some tea in."

Florence Nightingale rides again.

"What's James doing?"

"He's making dinner. Do you like pasta?"

"I don't know."

"Yes you do," she laughed. "You'll be all right. We'll make you some dinner. You don't have to eat it if you don't want to." She got out of bed. "See you soon."

I looked at the ceiling, shell-shocked. It was already starting to get dark. Tracey came back with the flowers falling out of a beer glass. She cleared a space on the dressing table and turned the glass this way and that. Water slopped out of the glass onto my makeup.

"That's my makeup."

"Sorry," she said, not noticing that the water had soaked through a letter and was pooling around my watch. "There." She looked at me expectantly.

"I moved some stuff into my mother's last night," she said.

I sat up and looked at my hand again. I didn't know what I was going to tell Liz. Maxine had probably already told her I was tripping. Maybe I should get up. I got out of bed southern-belle style, swooning as vertigo and stomach cramps hit.

"Did you hear me?"

"Sorry?" I said, clutching my stomach.

"I asked if you were going to come to the wedding. It's this weekend. What's the matter?"

"I feel terrible."

"Lie down then," she said, annoyed.

"OK." I crept back to the bed, doubled up and sweating.

"Well? Will you come to the wedding with me?"

"All right," I moaned. "God I feel terrible."

I groaned from beneath the full weight of my own paranoia. I straightened up again, staring blankly at the duvet. Tracey came over and hugged me. For a moment I adopted my small child gets squashed by moustachioed Aunty pose, and then sunk into her, clinging on for dear life.

"Let's go to bed," she whispered, pushing me back down onto it.

"*Tracey*."

"I can't help it... I really like you."

"Look," I took hold of her hand. "Thanks for coming over, and the flowers. I appreciate it –"

"Do you?" she said in the baby voice.

"Yeah," I said, wondering what the fuck I was doing.

Too late: she was gazing at me adoringly.

"Thank you," she said, and kissed my lips. "I –"

"Come on, let's get the tea." I picked up my blanket and pulled her weakly towards the door.

"But I was going to say something –"

"Come on." I hobbled through to the lounge, pulling her along after me, and collapsed onto the couch. "I'm just going to lie down here for a second. My hand hurts."

James came out of his bedroom.

"What happened to you last night?" he said.

"I don't want to talk about it."

"*Ooooh.*"

"Fuck off."

"*Ruth,*" Tracey said.

"Leave me alone," I said. "Both of you."

I flipped over and pressed my nose against the couch. Saliva dripped out of my mouth, making a wet spot on the upholstery. James and Tracey went into the kitchen and I could hear the martyred rattling of pots and pans, and then the door closed so I wouldn't be able to hear them talking about me. I undid the knot on the torn piece of sheet and looked at my hand. Fuck I was stupid. How dumb was it, going into work this morning? Thirty-four years old and still dropping trips; presently lying on the couch in this disgusting little flat with a mashed hand and a girlfriend I didn't particularly like.

> Tracksuit Man, Tracksuit Man,
> Tracksuit Man gonna catch me if he can
> He is out there wai – *ting!*
> And antici – pa – *ting!*
> That I'll make him a really happy man
> Yeah, I'll make him a really happy man

(sing it to the tune of Postman Pat)

11: Overload

"How many should I take?" James said, working out the price he could get for the rest. They were kneeling by Tracey's handbag looking at a sheet of small green and white pills.

"Have two."

"Thanks love," James said, and hung around until it was clear that that was all he was going to get, then, pocketing the pills, he went back to the kitchen, refusing to look at me. Tracey remained kneeling by her bag, looking furtively in my direction on the couch.

"Dinner's nearly ready."

"I'm not that hungry."

"We're making you pasta!"

"I'm not very hungry thanks."

"You should eat."

"Why? It's not mandatory is it?"

"You should try Prozac."

"Should I?"

"*Yes*. What's so funny about that?"

"Everyone's on it, aren't they?"

"*So?* Maybe everyone's depressed."

"Well, I suppose I'd better have some then."

She looked at me reproachfully.

"All right," I said, "what does it do?... Come on, tell me."

"It's very good," she said getting back *on* that horse. "I didn't realise until I started taking it." She took another sheet out of her bag. "Take the Monday one now, then take one every day. Sometimes it can take a few weeks to work."

"I can't just take yours –"

"I've got three months' worth. You can have a month, and then you can go to a doctor."

"A doctor's not going to give me Prozac just like that."

"Yes they will. Tell them you've moved."

"... If I have one now, will it make any difference?"

"Have two. You'll feel better."

"*Two?* What will that do?"

"It blocks off your emotional responses so you don't feel depressed."

"It hasn't blocked off your emotional responses."

"If you'd seen me before you wouldn't say that." She looked down at her bag.

"That's true."

I managed to gather together some saliva and force the pills down my throat. "What's on TV?" I said, lying back on the couch.

This gave her something concrete to get her teeth into, and she was also clearly delighted that I'd joined her in Prozac heaven: she scooted around the room looking for the remote control and switched the TV on. Some wildlife programme was on.

"Did you make the tea?" I said.

"*No.* I'll make it in a minute. How are you feeling now?"

"Awful."

She lifted my legs up and sat on the couch, fussing around with the blanket and arranging my legs over hers. "*Now.* What happened to your hand?"

"I don't know, I hurt it against a wall."

"*Oh no –*"

I checked to see if she was taking the piss, but it appeared she wasn't.

"– How did you do that?"

"I don't know. I just hurt it."

She held my foot in her hand, playing with my toes. "Oh dear."

"Mm. Is there some tea?"

"I'm not your slave," she said, massaging my toes.

"Why not? You'd make a good slave." I tapped her crotch with the ball of my foot.

"Hey –" She smiled and swung her legs onto the couch so that mine sat between the top of hers. I wiggled my big toe.

"That's nice," she said, and manoeuvred herself so that we were in a scissor configuration, moving her toes around politely until her foot was in the same position as mine. Our knees made a little tent out of the blanket and I could see her head above it. She was wearing leggings and no knickers by the feel of it. Her cunt was warm and squashy and it started to get damp as I moved my toes in time with hers. I used my big toe to push the fabric of her leggings inside her.

"Take your knickers off," she said.

I didn't want to look at her face – her eyes – so I kept my gaze at chin height while she rolled her leggings down, and I did as I was told. We got back into position.

"I thought you were sick," she said, smiling and placing her foot onto me again.

"I am."

She pushed against me, seesawed against me; her mouth's open and I can feel my own toe sticky inside her, I can feel her wet pubic hair I'm fucking her with my toe watching her face now it's so fucking erotic show me your cunt you dirty bitch I want to see you come Oh My

"Tea's made –"

James came waltzing in with a tray and we both froze.

"– And *what* are you two doing under there?"

"Nothing." I dislodged my foot and scanned the floor for my knickers which were poking out from the edge of the blanket. Tracey flapped the blanket so that it covered them. James stared openly in the hope of seeing something genital and knelt before us, pouring the tea.

"*Thank you* James," I said.

"That's OK love," he said, and sniffed the air appreciatively. "Ooh, my tummy's rumbling," he said to Tracey.

"Are you going now?" I asked.

"There's no need to be like that love," he said, giving Tracey her tea. "*Is* there Tracey?"

"Don't worry about him," Tracey said after he'd gone.

"He wanted to go to bed with me last night."

"James!" she said, nearly dropping her cup. "He's gay!"

"He'd fuck anything." I said, getting up and putting my knickers back on.

"Hey! I was enjoying that," she said.

"Were you? Would you like to see my tits?"

Her eyes buckled slightly and she put her tea down.

"OK."

I was wearing my pyjama top with nothing on underneath. I stood over her and lifted it slowly, giving her a glimpse of breast and then dropping it again, then reaching beneath it to squeeze my tits. I could see the outline of her hand masturbating under the blanket while she watched me. I pulled my shirt up and licked the forefinger on my good hand and dabbed it onto each nipple, pinching my nipples and pulling them out and then licking my finger again. I watched her as she came, it was quite fascinating: her face screwed up like she was constipated and she closed her eyes and pushed her bottom lip out and grimaced furiously like an ape. I let my top drop as she opened her eyes.

"All right?"

"Yeah." She jiggled further down the couch and spread her legs.

"What are you doing?" I asked, astonished.

"Coming again," she said, glancing at me and then getting stuck in, her hips bouncing up and down beneath the blanket, face contorted, chin jutting. James came in carrying a French stick and a bowl of salad and Tracey went limp and rolled over, pulling the blanket with her. James gave me a supercilious look before leaving the room. Prick. I went after him.

"I'm busy at the moment," he said when he saw me come in. "Do we have any Parmesan?" He flung open the fridge door and looked inside. "There's never anything in this house when you need it." I was standing in the doorway and he went to push past me. *"Excuse* me," he said.

I'd never had an argument with James before: mostly it had been light sarcasm – nothing as palpable as the controlled air of aggression that now filled the kitchen.

"No," I said.

"Get out of my way." He banged into me.

I blanched and peeled off down the hall, feeling vulnerable in my pyjama top and bare feet. Tracey was folding up the blanket. "What's going on?" she said, looking towards the front door which had just slammed shut.

"Nothing. Just that stupid fuck."

"Who? James?"

"Yes, *James.*"

"He's nice."

"Is he? And how would you know?"

"What does that mean?"

"Just what I said. I'm the one who lives here."

"Don't you want me to be here?"

"What? Why does everything have to be about you?"

"It isn't. It's always about you."

"What are you talking about?"

"Well it is always about you. You don't care about me."

"Tracey –"

"It's true. You don't care about me. At least James does."

"What?"

"You're always hassling him. He –"

"You don't know anything about him. You don't even know him."

She hung her head, looking at the blanket.

"Are you crying?"

"No."

"Yes you are."

"I'm not! Stop it!"

"I'm not *doing* anything," I said. "Don't be such a victim."

She looked at me incredulously.

"I'm not a victim."

"Yes you are."

"No I'm not!" She sat down on the couch and clutched the folded blanket to her chest. "Nobody loves me."

"Don't be ridiculous!" I took the blanket off her. "They're all fucking well after you."

"But I don't *huh huh* want them... *I want you.*"

"I don't know why," I said, flattery mixing with mild revulsion for her.

"I do." She stood up and wrapped herself firmly around me in what was now becoming a familiar manner. "I love you."

I didn't say anything; I stood there silently overwhelmed by everything, trying to stop my sore hand from being crushed, and trying not to appear too cruel. And to be honest I quite liked the attention from her: if at times it was cloying, it was at others flattering and convenient. I stroked her hair. "We're both a mess."

"Nyeah." She held on to me tightly.

James came in with the dinner and found us standing in that position.

"Did you get the Parmesan?" I said, gagging on several large globules of pride.

"Yum!" Tracey looked at me gratefully and bounded over to the table like a child determined to be good and loaded up her plate with pasta, while James avoided eye contact with me and offered Tracey salad and French bread, pleased with his own efforts – which to him would constitute an excuse not to cook for another six months. I went and got dressed and sat in the armchair with my plate on my lap, watching TV while they chit-chatted, both glancing at me every so often. There was a shot of a hedgehog on TV burrowing into a pile of compost, and a woman's voice saying that you had to be careful with hedgehogs because they found cosy spots to hibernate for the winter where they would remain soundly asleep until spring. I sat up in my chair. It was the middle of winter now and I'd seen the hedgehog by my car, when? Two weeks ago? I felt – this sounds weird – but I felt... *lonely*.

James and Tracey blurred into the background and my ears filled with the sound of the sea – not a roaring, waves-crashing-on-beach, seagulls-squalling sound, but one that was similar to holding a shell to your ear: a slight aural twist on reality which scared me. Maybe I hadn't done that to the hedgehog at all; maybe it was all a hallucination of some sort. I'd taken that same acid twice now and both times I'd seen the guy in the tracksuit. Maybe he wasn't real at all. But he had to be real. I knew exactly what he looked like. About six foot, watery blue eyes, straggly white hair tinged with yellow and parted in the middle; wearing a dirty grey tracksuit. Looked like a deranged hippy.

And I *had* killed the hedgehog because... well, because... I did. I'd been doing that sort of shit on and off since I was about nine and Ricky Forster put my frog through one of those old washing machine wringers at the school swimming pools. Me and Ricky were round by the changing sheds watching the frog hop around on the concrete and Ricky suddenly said *watch this* and he scooped the frog up and ran over to the wringer and put one of its legs between the rollers and turned the handle. I ran after him and watched as the frog flailed about with one leg in the roller, and then Ricky wrenched the handle and its head went through, its eyes bulging and then squirting open. Ricky screamed and ran off, leaving me standing there with the frog dangling halfway through the rollers. There didn't seem much point in rescuing him so I reached for the handle and turned it slowly until his stomach blew up like a small football, and then, *pip*, through he went.

Ricky and I made a pact not to tell anyone. We would stare at each other with bright scared eyes, and I would always say no, let's go for a ride, or let's go to the pools, but in the end I always did it. Next we went for one of the Forsters' kittens – he said it had cat flu anyway – and put it under the big concrete roller on the tennis courts, which caused restrained hysteria amongst the mothers the next day who rightly surmised that one roll wouldn't have killed it, couldn't possibly have made *that amount of mess*; then my guinea pig, Squeak, with its legs tied to pieces of string with nails attached to the end of them. We laid it across the railway line and hammered the nails into the ground and watched it struggling to get free while we waited for the next train. I was going to save it. I was behind the railway sheds lying with my face flat to the gravel nearly sick for Squeak, *Squeak!*, but a train came along before I could. I hated Ricky for that. He said *it was your idea poo head* and rode off and left me there. There was a bit of a break for a while and then after that we used mice. We never ran out of them, and my parents never asked what had happened to them. They were always getting killed anyway. My father would sit on one and squash it when I was playing with them on the couch, or my mother would flatten one under the foot of her sewing machine. They didn't care. *Don't bring the bloody things in here then.*

Ricky moved away when I was about ten and I didn't do it again. Not until after I'd left home – I was eighteen – and I'd been ill in bed for a few days, just lying there staring at the trees through the window, thinking too hard, and I got up and rang work and said I was feeling better and would come in that afternoon. Before I left for work I went to a pet shop and bought a rabbit and a hutch, and left them out on the back lawn, and for days I'd look at the hutch through my window and think *go, go out and feed it!* but I didn't.

I always felt sick with this secret – not just the rabbit, but all of it; I felt sick *doing it*, but it gave me some sort of control somehow. It frightened me too, because at the back of my mind there was this thought that I was blanking a whole lot of other stuff out. Something. I didn't try to analyse it, because if I did I began to feel like there was a *landfill* stinking under the carpet, not just a few odds and ends that could be cleared up with a small brush and pan.

"What happened to Polly?" I said.

Tracey stopped eating. "She's at my mother's. Why?"

"Why don't you bring her back here?"

"No! You wouldn't look after her."

It was weak protest: I could tell she was hoping I was going to ask *her* to stay too.

"You could move in here for a while if you like," I said. "We've got a spare bed."

"... Yeah but I haven't got any money."

"Don't worry about it, we're paying rent anyway."

"I don't mind," James said, his fork poised in front of him, eyeing her up for some twisted reason of his own. Bait probably. For the straight boys.

I got up, holding my uneaten dinner. "I'll do the dishes," I said.

James looked at Tracey and sniggered.

"*What?*"

"The pills are working then?" he said.

They probably were actually. I was feeling quite active: still tired, but nothing like I was an hour ago. A *minute* ago.

"Do you think they would have worked this quickly?"

"You'd definitely notice it," Tracey said. "You seem much better."

The phone rang. Please let it be Martin.

It was some gayboy for James. Tracey helped me take the dishes out to the kitchen. She looked around the kitchen proprietorially while I thought about Martin.

"I'll do the dishes," she said. "You won't be able to do them with your hand."

"Do you want me to help?"

"No, you sit down. Do we have any coffee?"

"Yes, *we* do."

"If you don't want me to stay I won't." She folded her arms.

"No. Don't be silly. Here you are." I got the coffee for her.

"You run hot and cold don't you?" she said, filling up the kettle.

"Why, what do you mean?"

"Well one minute you're all over me, then you're – you're –"

"What?"

"Well, you're – I don't know – do you want me to move in?"

"I wouldn't have asked you if I didn't want you to."

"Mm," she said, unconvinced. "I don't think you know what you want."

"Don't you, indeed?" I stood behind her and rubbed her bottom. "I do."

Her buttocks twitched happily and she leaned back into me, letting the water spill over the top of the kettle. Into the element socket, I noted.

(Things were going a bit fast, but then they always did at the beginning of relationships. You jumped in, boots and all; it was only later you found yourself scrabbling up the walls of the pit; tin opener dropped next to the pile of worms swiftly untangling themselves in the dirt below.)

Needless to say she slept in my bed that night – already lumped under the duvet when I returned from the bathroom, feigning indifference with her back to me. She could have been dead for all I knew. I fell asleep before I could find out, lying close to the cliff and spending most of the night rolling over and over, trying to adjust to having someone else in my bed. Whenever I got comfortable she'd come sneaking across the sheets towards me, nestling in with a couple of casual sniffs. Then her hand would creep over the trenches and down onto my stomach, where it would settle uneasily.

My own hand was throbbing; I got up at about three to take some painkillers. When I came back to bed, even though she was awake Tracey said nothing. She was crammed up against the wall until I got in, then after a moment she rolled over and the arm came creeping over again.

I lay there regretting my decision to ask her to move in. But I wasn't even sure if it was my decision. Did other people's minds work in the same way mine did? Sort of automatically?

I fell back into another restless sleep, dreaming of nothing, and when I woke next morning Tracey was lying close to me, looking at my face.

"What's the matter?" I said.

"Nothing. I'm just looking at you."

"Why?"

"You're funny." She smiled and stroked my cheek. "Funny girl."

"You can use my toothbrush if you want," I said, looking at my hand to see what had happened to it overnight.

"You are *so rude*," she said between closed teeth.

"No I'm not. You haven't brought yours have you?"

"No..."

"Well then, you can use mine."

"Thanks."

"That's OK."

I don't know what sort of perverse pleasure I was getting out of these interactions – none really – but it was kind of interesting to see how far I could go. I pretended I'd banged my hand against something.

"*Ow*. I'd better get up," I said. "What are you doing today?"

"I'm going to pick up my things. Is it all right if I use the car? I'll get Polly while I'm there. Do you like cats though? I thought you didn't?" She hunkered down under the duvet and smiled up at me.

I wanted to use the car myself. Maybe go round and see Martin. "Are you going to stay tonight then?" I said.

She hurled back the duvet and attempted to launch herself out of bed, which proved to be rather difficult as she was still on the inside against the wall. As she climbed over me I got a close-up of bottom flesh and pubic hair.

She sat silently on the edge of the bed and pulled on her leggings, her shoulders hunched away from me. Her body out of clothes was nothing like it was in. When you unwrapped the present all you got was a slab of meat; a slab of pale meat with a pretty face, lying there, waiting to absorb you.

Overload.

"Where's my Prozac?" I said.

"I don't know."

"Will you find it for me?"

"*No.*" She finished getting dressed and left the room, returning with the pills and a glass of water.

"Save some water for me," she said, handing me the glass belligerently.

I'd forgotten we were both on it.

For a drug that purportedly stifled one's emotional responses, there was a good deal of high drama going on.

I put it down to being bisexual and headed for the shower.

12: The wedding

And so it goes. Or so it went. It's not at all difficult to remember the week she moved in, what with the trip at the start of it and the wedding on the Saturday. The wedding. Oh yeah. How could I possibly forget the wedding? Even though it wasn't just one thing, but a series of events that culminated in what happened, what happened at the wedding still haunts me. When my life flashes before my eyes – if it's going to – I hope they've edited out the piece on the wedding.

You'll have to cut the wedding scene mate – we're running a bit over at the moment.

It's unlikely that they will cut it out because it's pretty *lurid*. Compulsive viewing. Fly on the wall stuff. And all of it significant. For me at least, because it all led to this. This period of complete... nothingness. Except for writing this, and my visits from Ray (Dee doesn't come any more), and my weekly excursions to the library, which climax in a cup of coffee and piece of cheesecake on the way back to the car. I've noticed I'm getting a lot of pimples these days. I didn't realise you got pimples this far down the track. It's the sugar probably – I have three sugars in my coffee now. Or maybe it's all the shit I'm eating. I'll buy a whole roasted chicken at the supermarket and take it home and eat it till I feel sick, or I'll scoff back five chocolate eclairs in one sitting. And the biscuits! Christ. Chocolate chip and hazelnut, rich shortbread, toffee clusters – at least a packet a day, sometimes more. I never used to eat so much crap. It could be hormones I suppose – bored shitless on their dull march around my body, clutching their drooping placards: *Have Children. Now.*

I'm constantly reminded of mortality. I go out thinking I look OK until I catch a glimpse of myself in a shop window and see the decay. My face is finally caving in. I look old. My mouth looks like an arsehole, and I've stopped wearing lipstick.

I've found another place I really like – a picture of it anyway. I soaked the label off a wine bottle and stuck it up on the wall. It's from South Africa: a vineyard situated on the banks of the Breede River, 15km from Robertson, on the road to Bonnievale. The little painting on the label is beautiful: red flowers in the foreground, in front of two low sheds tucked beneath yellow and brown hills you could be at the top of in ten minutes. It's sweet and summery.

Back here, the weather's changing to autumn: startling blue skies and clear. *Clear.* All the shit moved along.

"Oh," a woman's voice said. "There you are Tracey."

A beanbag in its Sunday best was listing our way. This could not possibly be Tracey's mother... Could it?

Tracey tried not to look, but even she couldn't help it. She'd spent the week dropping hints that her mother would come as a shock – at one stage trying to maintain she was adopted – but I wasn't prepared for this. Mrs Tracey looked like an obese Labrador let out of the garden shed unexpectedly, a wreath of dry curls framing her mushroomy face. She didn't look *specifically* like Tracey, but parts of her did: the shape of the mouth; the eyes were the same.

And (*oh, joy!*) it looked like she was going to try and hug Tracey. I stepped back, smiling, and Tracey grabbed my arm and shoved me into her mother with a *this is Ruth*. Resisting the push I pivoted lightly into her mother's shoulder, holding my hand awkwardly in the air to stop it from being banged. Somehow we managed a round of semi-dignified hellos, Tracey pouting like a teenager.

The three of us were standing in the churchyard with about twenty other people, most of whom were now looking at us; one man in a cherry red suit ogling Tracey's legs. It was the right sort of day to get married: a light blue sky with several jet trails strung across it adding to the marital gaiety of it all.

"This is nice," I said, indicating her mother's skirt. It wasn't, but I had to say something before I pushed Tracey into the fence.

"Is it?" she asked hopefully. "It's not too much?"

"No it's lovely. Did you make it?"

"No..." she said, looking down at it. "How are you Tracey?"

Tracey was looking the other way, distancing herself from the conversation as much as possible.

"Good," she said without turning around.

"When's – is it *Alison?* – arriving?" I asked.

"Oh. She's coming in the car with Gordon."

"That's good," I said.

"*Where's* Gordon?" Tracey said.

"In the car."

"I hope you're not sitting with us –"

"*Tracey*," I said.

We stood there in silence until her mother said, "Do you have any brothers and sisters, Ruth?"

"No she doesn't," Tracey said. "You should go in."

"I suppose I should, I –"

"No, you stay with us," I said. "We're going in in a minute."

Tracey stood beside me morosely, trying to work out what to do next.

At least the Prozac was working. I felt like I'd been escorted to the front of my brain; been plucked out of the mud and placed on dry land; showered and changed and given a cup of hot cocoa. I wasn't thinking about anything much. Not *in depth* anyway. Information entered and went somewhere. The only side effects so far were feeling dizzy and not eating – but I wasn't worried about them, I *noticed* them. I was aware that I was on heavy-duty chemicals however: that was obvious.

There hadn't been any problems with Liz either. I bought a proper bandage for my hand and walked in the next day as if nothing had happened. Maxine was ready for scandal, sitting up in her chair when she saw me. I glanced at her and said *hi* and carried on up the stairs.

Liz was on the phone and looked at my hand first, then at my face, all the time chatting away to somebody about her holiday. *Perfect. Sun sea and sex – you should try it. Hahahahaha.* (Sex would have amounted to doing it with the barman once, maybe twice if he could face it, if he was drunk enough.) She wasn't interested in me anyway – what had happened to my hand – she was much more interested in her: who had called her; who had written to her; what had been said about her. Then we had the photos: Liz on the beach in a black one-piece and wide-brimmed hat; Liz on a moped; Liz on a moped in a sarong with her arms around Paolo; Liz in a hotel room, Paolo on the balcony in an open-necked shirt and tight jeans, brandishing a beer bottle. (Tourists, garage mechanics, waiters, had all been seconded into taking these pictures; given a token smile as she took the camera off them to check the number of photos left, carefully closing the lens cover ready for the next good time.) After the photos we got the presents: I got a brown vinyl donkey with a mane of what looked suspiciously like cat hair, and there were the usual trinkets and cigarettes and T-shirts. By midday she was tired of being nice to people and snapped out a *yes it was very nice thank you* when Mace asked how it went, then picked up the phone to avoid any further discussion with him. (Liz didn't have time for Mace unless he was doing something for her. Then she was in and out of his office all day, backwards and forwards hail fellow well met, until the job was done. It always took her months to pay the bill as well, because she knew she could keep him waiting.)

On the home front, Tracey had moved her stuff in, bringing Polly with her. The spare room wasn't big enough to hold it all, and now the hall was jammed with rickety pot-plant stands, and china cabinets with the glass missing, and old posters, and grubby cushions, and plastic bags splitting open with cassettes.

She'd continued to sleep in my bed, my own room steadily filling up with her things: dusty fabric roses growing in the hinges of the dressing table mirror, next to postcards of glamorous women in passionate clinches (with each other), and great swathes of clothes hanging over my door so that it didn't close properly, hanging off the end of the bed, thrown in the corner, piled on the chair, stuffed in laundry baskets, and abseiling down the sides of dirty rucksacks. I couldn't believe the amount of stuff she had: rubbish bags full of old ball gowns; shoe-boxes of fingernail polish and perfume and eye-liner; and knickers coming out of her ears: all with ribbons or bows or chocolate fish, or some such enticement hanging off them.

There was also the small matter of the cat, which she'd insisted on keeping in the bedroom. I'd come across her several times scrabbling around cleaning up after it, hoping I hadn't noticed the saucers of dried jellymeat and curdled milk hidden behind the door.

I didn't really care to be honest. It all felt short-term. I'd started making a mental note of what to take with me when I moved, and had even begun to think about the possibility of moving in with Martin. I hadn't told Tracey about him yet. I hadn't spoken to him anyway. His answerphone had been on all week and I'd driven past his place on Thursday night, and again on Friday, but it was all in darkness.

The only immediate problem was my hand, which didn't seem to be healing properly. There was pus coming out of the scabs. I'd taken to swallowing two painkillers every morning with my Prozac, and thinking that maybe I should go to the doctor for some antibiotics, but I hadn't got round to it. I put a new bandage over it for the wedding, and nursed it against my waist to shelter it from any bangs and bumps.

Tracey wanted me to wear a sling. She'd decked me out in a green woollen suit of hers, a pair of thick black tights, and put my hair up in bobby clips. After she'd finished with me she went to work on herself, listening to her compilation cassettes of gay icons who weren't gay, and tossing her clothes around and dancing with the cat. She finally decided on a diaphanous knee-length peacock-blue gown, blue fingernail polish with glitter in it, and a beaded Victorian purse hanging off one arm.

She was poking around in the purse now. "I'm going to the toilet," she said and went off in search of one.

The guy in the cherry red suit craned his neck around his wife to see where she was going and saw me watching him and pretended he was looking for someone else.

"I suppose you know everybody here – ?" I said to Tracey's mother. "Um, what shall I call you?"

"Oh. I'm Faye."

"Faye. Hi."

"Hi." She said it like it was a foreign language, and smoothed her giant skirt.

We stood there watching people arrive, not saying much. Tracey eventually appeared from the side of the church and acted as if her mother wasn't there, coming up to me and holding my arm and smiling at me, so close I could have touched her lips with my tongue. Her mother looked away, and got a handkerchief out of her handbag.

"Come on, let's go in," Tracey said loudly and several people turned to look at her. Cherry Red got ready to jockey for position. We crunched our way into the church, Tracey still holding my arm, and her mother swaying along beside us. We let her mother go through the door first. Tracey pointed at her bloated bottom and I frowned and nudged her with my elbow.

It seemed impossible that I'd only known Tracey for a few weeks. She was like an annoying younger sister. A week ago I had no intention of talking to her again and now here she was – living with me. I looked at her mother who was trying to get comfortable on the narrow bench beside us. I felt I knew *her* as well.

It was nice being in church. The air smelt of newly cut flowers and candle smoke and virginity. Oh yeah, and *death*. The groom was rocking himself quietly up the front, next to the best man. Tracey sniffed.

"Did you have a line?" I whispered.

"Yeah." She was all eyes for a moment, and then smiled and started singing along to the music on the PA.

"That was for later," I said.

She squeezed my arm and snuggled up to me, moving her hips around and clicking her fingers. Cherry Red was trying to get into the row directly behind us, but his wife was indicating some empty seats closer to the front. He followed her reluctantly, nodding at us as he went. A man was handing out embossed programmes. *The Wedding of Brian David Campbell and Alison Meekle. Programme.* I skipped the vows and Corinthians quote to see where the reception was being held. The Cedars. 12.15pm. Speeches 1.30pm.

I couldn't get a good look at Brian: he was looking straight ahead saying a silent prayer for himself, shaking his leg like an athlete before the big race. The vicar arrived, suitably solemn, belly full, and the music did a slow fade to silence and the *Wedding March* began.

Tracey's mother stood up again (which was notable for the effort it required). Like fat people universally she tried to make it look easy, gripping the pew in front of us with both hands to give herself some extra leverage. My eye was drawn to her waist area; she looked like she had a huge, partially deflated beach ball under her skirt.

Meanwhile, on the other side of me, Tracey was revelling in her own gorgeousness, clinging onto my arm and watching for Alison.

Alison. Right. It'd be interesting to see what type Tracey went for. (Besides me that is, and I had no idea what type I was. Shithead? Complete arsehole?)

Alison came down the aisle in full wedding regalia; Gordon, her weather-beaten father out of step beside her. Alison was wearing a veil so I couldn't her face properly, but she had short streaked hair and big sporty teeth. I looked at Tracey (*you fucked that?*). She'd even got her mother to fork out for some *lingerie* for a wedding present. A red slip which she'd wrapped in tissue paper, and then tied an antique red satin bow around it and sprinkled tiny red stars all over it. She'd left the glue and packet of stars on my dressing table: now everything was covered in stars, and when you put your hand to your face, small red stars remained there and you had to get your fingernail beneath them before they would come off. Tracey loved them, flicking them all over the floor like the fairy godmother. Maybe that's how she saw herself? The benevolent, all giving Tracey. All loving. Selectively. She certainly wasn't all loving towards her mother.

I wondered why her mother wasn't sitting up the front with the immediate family. Alison's real mother was up there: you couldn't miss her with her tennis racket teeth and new blue hat.

Alison spoke well, clearly promising to love honour and obey, and the best man dropped the ring at one stage – it fell into Brian's trouser cuff. They both saw it: Brian had been watching his trouser cuff since they started, only lifting his head to mumble that, no, he would never want to punch her when he was drunk, that he would never want to fuck her best friend, that he would always agree with her, and would endeavour to remain in his twenties with hair and ambitions.

I was dying for a line, although the Prozac was helping things along, but I probably shouldn't have been taking two a day.

Brian and Alison said *I do* and things moved quickly from there. Alison kissed everyone on the way back down the aisle, and our row filed out. Someone let Tracey's mother out. I stood there for a while letting people go past.

"Come on," Tracey said, pushing me in the small of the back.

"Hold on."

She kept nudging me forward until I bumped into Cherry Red who made way for us and then moved in close behind Tracey. When we got out of the church Tracey went straight over to see Alison and I stopped and leaned against the church door, watching her. Relatives milled around saying hello and shaking hands, the smaller ones pushing through the leggy undergrowth. Brian and Alison were having their photo taken, and several people with video cameras were leaning around trees and zooming in from flower beds. I could see Tracey's mother standing by the official party, being ignored by the look of it. Gordon was having his photo taken with Alison. He looked like he was more suited to being strapped into a wheelhouse, the trawler heeling into the wind. *She's bloody rough out here. Make us a tea.*

Tracey's mother had *enormous* tits. She had enormous everything. I wondered how much food you'd have to eat to get that size. That gland thing was bullshit. *Food* did that. Fucking awful outfit. Actually, put her in some jeans and a white shirt and she'd make a good dyke.

Tracey was kissing Alison and patting Brian and the parents, having her photo taken with them. Glamorous girl joins wedding party; Gordon pulls at collar, wondering how much diesel he's got on board.

Tracey noticed me watching her and came over.

"Come and meet Alison."

"I'd rather have a line. Can I have it?" I said, indicating her bag.

"They've only got a few more photos to take, then they're leaving."

"Doesn't your mother get on with them or something?"

"No."

"Why not?"

"I don't know."

"Doesn't the real mother like her?"

"I don't know, the sister or something."

"Which one?"

She pointed to a woman who was pushing a little girl along by her shoulders. *Move. Now.*

"I can't believe you slept –"

"Well I did, so shut up."

"Can I have that please?" I took the bag off her and went to find the toilet. A few people were standing around smoking, and the vicar was waiting at the side door, looking harassed.

"It might never happen," I said.

"No," he said, annoyed, as if a hundred people said this to him every day. "And it very well might." He banged on the door.

I laughed as I walked towards the corner of the building. "It was just an idle comment."

"And the devil makes work for idle hands," he snapped back.

"Does he?" I said, wishing I'd never started this.

"So I believe." He thumped the door again. *"Helen."*

Humourless prick. Backstage at the vicarage eh. For some reason I'd imagined carnation talcum powder and a ginger cat. It was all Fantasyland anyway. God and the devil. How could you believe that crap?

Shit. Dead end.

"Can you show me where the toilets are please?"

He looked smug and pointed me in the right direction. The door he was banging on opened and a woman with a white pudding-bowl haircut stood there. As I walked off I heard him saying impatiently to her, *Is there something wrong with that door?* and then, *I asked you to turn the photocopier on,* before the door smacked shut again.

It took me ten minutes to open Tracey's bag with one hand and then cut out the coke; I didn't really need it, it wasn't even midday. It was good though; it gave everything an extra edge; made everything feel just that little bit more important as I stepped back past the church.

God my heart was going for it. Woo doggy.

Maybe sit down.

Shit. Jesus.

Drug overdose.

Until you've had a panic attack you're never fully acquainted with fear. You might have passed it in the street, you might even be able to say what it was wearing – colours and so forth – but you don't really *know it* until it's throttled the shit out of you so many times that just the sound of its key in the door makes you want to piss your pants. You might know the moment. It's you standing at the water's edge realising your kid's been out of sight for two minutes; it's the footsteps of a serial rapist thumping up behind you in the park, in the dark; it's having less than a minute to inflate the life raft and you're submerged upside-down in the galley with your leg snapped in half.

Except it's *sustained*: it's that moment again and again and again; it explodes and then explodes and then explodes, feeding off itself, and there is no justification for it: there are no rapists, no boat, no kiddy. And so we pant and sweat and clutch at our collars and run to the toilets and lock ourselves in – because the fear, which is solely responsible for the racing heart, the shaking and sweating and choking, the fear has no basis, it's a mental aberration, which surely only happens to... *mad people?*

"Ruth, are you in there?"

"Sorry?"

"What are you doing in there?"

"Um, I'm not feeling very well."

"Why, what's the matter?"

"Nothing. I'll see you outside in a minute."

"Everyone's gone –"

"Yeah sorry. I won't be long. Wait by the car."

"What are you doing in there?"

"Nothing."

After she'd gone I looked into the toilet for a while, and then forced myself to open the door. I got to the car somehow; Tracey was in the driver's seat.

"Are you all right?"

"Do you mind not talking to me?"

Tracey roared off to The Cedars like an ambulance driver. She got lost and had to run into a shop and ask directions; by the time we arrived I was feeling slightly better, less *heart* oriented anyway.

"Are you all right now?"

"Yeah. Let's have a drink. Can you get it?"

She did her hair in the mirror and licked her lips before jumping out of the car, a carefree study in peacock blue. I scurried inside after her.

The Cedars was typical wedding fodder: miniature lily pond, wooden bridge, swing with a red bow tied to it, nose-catching pot-pourri in the toilets – which featured framed photos of all the happy twosomes on the bridge, at the swing. The whole place smelt of multiple vacuum cleanings. Tracey's mother was standing near the window by herself, looking over at us.

"Why is your mother by herself?"

"I don't want to talk to my mother!"

"I'll go and get her."

"*No.*"

"Why not?" I beckoned her mother over.

Faye waddled up to us and put her bag on the floor. "Did you two come the long way?"

"Yeah," I said, about to say we'd got lost when Tracey piped up, "Ruth was freaking out in the toilets."

"My hand," I said, "I hurt it –"

"Tripping," Tracey said.

"Would you like a drink?" I said. "Wine, or – ?"

"Shall I get it?" her mother asked anxiously.

"No, I'll get it," Tracey said, and walked off.

We talked about Alison's dress, and the cat, and how Tracey always had a cat, even when she was little. Tracey came back with our drinks and disappeared into the crowd again. Her mother and I watched Alison gliding about with a tray of canapés, smiling toothily. Tracey's mother was keeping up with me: whenever my glass was empty so was hers. After the third glass I excused myself and popped out to the phone.

"Is that *Martin?* It's Ruth."

"Right."

"What do you mean, *right?*" I laughed. "I'm at a wedding."

"Yeah?"

"How are you?"

"Good. I have to go. Somebody's waiting for me."

"Where are you going?"

"Work."

"Oh well, have a good time," I said gaily (love interest, love object of Martin Myers).

"Yep."

"See you soon," I singsonged.

I hung up and then rang his number again.

"It's Ruth again. I'd like to talk to you."

"I have to go."

"OK. I'll call you tomorrow."

I put the phone down, just pissed enough, Class A, and prescription drugged enough, not to care.

– Bullshit, you fucking care all right. It's the Prozac that's putting it on hold.

– I *don't* care.

– You fucking do. Wait till the hall light's out.

– What do you mean by *that?*

– Just wait.

– No. *Mum! Mummy!*

Fucking Martin. I wasn't sure I liked Prozac anymore. It created a sense of occasion and then removed you from the room. Or maybe that was the alcohol. Or the line I'd had. I was starting to feel anxious again. I went over to the dining room. The Cedars staff were throwing cheap bottles of wine onto the tables, and Brian was looking at his speech notes. It all looked so... dull. These people were only famous for their *piercing laughs*, or their *persistent ear infections*, or their *moist Christmas cakes*. These people were the drones; the bones; the marrow of life. Fuck I was elitist. These were real people. I could learn a lot from these people. (Like what? Fucking what?)

There must be something.

I opened the main door and let myself out. Side paths led off into the ornamental garden. I said hello to a dog and walked down the path signposted The Stables. It led to the front of the building, which overlooked a big lawn. A horse was grazing near the fence. Through the windows I could see people gathering in the dining room. A door opened and Tracey came out, followed by Cherry Red and another couple. The wife wasn't with them: Cherry must have given her the slip. I watched them pick their way across the lawn, Tracey leading the way, charming the birds out of the trees in her splendid outfit. She approached the horse like a seasoned jockey, and stood there with its head embraced in one arm, smiling and chatting with her new admirers, horse included.

I left her to it and went back inside. My hand was beginning to ache; the painkillers must have worn off. I found an empty table and poured myself a glass of wine. Tracey's mother was standing by the main table with Alison and Gordon. Better try and act normal.

"Congratulations," I said walking up to them, thinking how stupid I looked, dressed up like a warped nanny, with my hand in a bandage.

"Don't forget, will you, Dad?" Alison said. She hiked up her dress and pole-vaulted off.

"This is Tracey's friend," Tracey's mother said. Eyes a tad too bright.

Gordon nodded at the lezzie. (Looks normal enough.)

"Nice to meet you," I said, feeling dizzy. "Um – I might sit down now –"

"I'll come with you, shall I?" Tracey's mother said, and went to follow me.

"Oh? Aren't you sitting with – ?"

"Oh. No, I –" She looked embarrassed. Gordon was looking in the opposite direction. Fuck knows what these two were up to. It was all fucked anyway. Everything.

"Come on," I said, and she lumbered after me to a table in the corner. She put her handbag on the chair beside her, saving a seat for Tracey. Tracey appeared at the door and looked around.

"Oh. Here she is now," her mother said, reaching for the wine. "Doesn't she look pretty in that blue?"

Tracey came up to the table, scowling. "*You're* not sitting here, are you?" she said to her mother.

"At least the weather's been good for them anyway," her mother said.

"Why aren't you sitting with Gordon?"

"Tracey," I said, "just sit down."

Her mother took her handbag off the chair next to her. "You know why, Tracey," she said, flustered, trying to get the chair out.

"Oh yeah, that's right – you *stole* Gordon away from them, didn't you?" Tracey laughed. "Where's my purse? Fuck."

"In the car," I said.

"Tracey, please don't swear," her mother said.

Tracey went to get her bag.

"Never mind," her mother said to me after she'd gone, intent on getting more liquid into her glass. "Life's not always fair, is it Ruth?"

"No," I said. Thanks for that.

"How are you two getting on anyhow?"

"OK."

(*Stop* looking at me like that.)

"You two – ?"

"Pardon?"

"You know," she said, looking at me over the top of her glass.

(No I don't think I do, and if I do, I don't think I want *you* to know.)

"I think the speeches are about to start," I said.

Grunty pants father said fuck all, Brian fiddled with his arse and proposed a toast, and Alison did everything by the book. She cut the cake and gobbled her chicken and apricots, and mingled and danced and included everybody except Faye and me. We drank. Our chicken and apricots were taken away untouched. Drink drink drinky drink until it all became a big swollen drunken thing tripping up the stairs talking loudly to everyone in the garden tell her to *shut up* drinky drinky drink. Drink. *Where's my drink?* Wanna dance? Drunk enough to fall out of the dining room with my arm stretched halfway around the back of Faye who was holding her broken shoe. Wrong room. Wrong door. Where's the toilet? My hand! Watch my hand! Hey! She crashes into some brooms. I can't pull her up. She's got my good hand, pulling me down, we're laughing hysterically, I'm falling onto her, bouncing off her chest, she pushes my face back into them and – there

I go, that's me by the mop bucket! – that's me, I'm the one latching onto those double obscenities like a hungry baby.

   – Cut this!

   – Fuck no. This is the best bit.

   – It'll never pass the censor. Keep it for the Christmas tape. Man, will you look at the size of that *bra*.

   Lock it. Lock the door!

   There's a monster in there!

   (And it wants to come out.)

13: We babies are otay now

It's the next day and we're at Martin's. Martin is at one end of the table and Tracey is at the other. Tracey is flirting with him. I mention my hangover, which is so immense I can hardly speak, and they look at each other like children with alcoholic parents. The flowers are still there. No evidence of a girlfriend in the kitchen. I stroke Tracey's hair as I'm passing. Martin understands now. (He is super friendly to me now.) Look at my new friend! (My *lover*) Isn't she gorgeous! Martin? Martin?

R: "You fancied him!"
T: "No I didn't!"
R: "You did."
T: "He was nice, I didn't *fancy* him."
R: "Why's that? You're *gay?*"
T: "*Yes.*"
R: "And you've never had a boyfriend?"
T: "No not really."
R: "Why do you like women then?"
T: "I don't know. Why do *you* like them?"
R: "*God I feel sick.*"
T: "Who is he anyway?"
R: "*I'm going to be sick.*"
T: "Good job."

"Tracey?"
"Yes."
"Hello."
"… Hello."
"Roll over here."

"No."

"I'm sorry. Kiss me? *Pease*."

"No. Where did you go with my mother at the wedding?"

"What?"

"With my mother? You were all over her."

"Your *mother?* She was pissed as a fart. What about you and that guy in the red suit?"

"Were you jealous?"

"Yes."

"*Ohh*. Poor Ruth…"

"Don't touch me."

"Don't be jealous. Come here."

"No."

"Come here. Good girl. *There*. Otay now?"

"Otay now."

We babies are *otay now*.

"Hold on, I just want to get something out from under the bed."

"What?"

"Close your eyes. It's a surprise."

14: An imbalance of carbon dioxide

I was thinking this morning that I'd like to fuck a rock star. In the lift on the way to his room. In the shower. In front of the mirror next to his guitar. Wherever. I don't mind: it's not the act itself that appeals, but the prospect of being caught up in the shallowness that swims with them, the excitement of being hustled from one of those pod-like cars into the hotel lobby. So I suppose what I really want is the sycophancy. The glory by association bit.

(But not the other bit. The bit by the tour bus and he's sprawled along the back seat, getting caught up in the rock star bit again, unable to stop himself. Fuck it, he *likes* being a rock star. Show time! What's he going to be today? Moody? Histrionic? *Nice?* Popping a lolly into his gob and not even thinking of looking down; down into the terrifying shadow of his own superstardom; down into the land of the giant tyres where you and your chicken legs quake with hope and embarrassment. Because rock stars don't wave goodbye, not unless they're clever – then not only are they rock stars but they're also *amazing*: every *please*, *thank you* and *excuse me* is pressed to the swelling breast of the stupefied recipient and spoken about in pubs, across pillowcases and around campfires for years afterwards. Rock stars always win. (No matter if they have just committed adultery. Or tried to.) I wonder what it would be like to fuck a woman rock star? I wonder if she'd wave? Bye! Seeya! *See You!*

Ray and I had something resembling sex yesterday. We were stoned, and he pulled aside his underpants just in time, and came on my stomach. (I know, disgusting, but I couldn't imagine him putting his cock inside me and I don't think he could either.) I don't even know why we did it. It's all cyclical I suppose: sometimes you're depressed, sometimes you're sexual, sometimes you're depressed. (You're never happy. Fuck no. That'd be too much to ask for.)

I read this story back this morning and that depressed the fuck out of me as well. I wish it was denser, not so *surface*. But that's me, yep, that's Ruth: a product of the times. The superficial miss.

I wonder how different it would be if I was a man? If I was a man there might be more *action* and less analysing going on.

Maybe I am? Maybe this is all a big riddle that I have to work out, and then, perfectly, at the end, a Snow White appears (could you jump into that red velvet gown for a moment Nastassja? That's it, the one with the black bodice) and kisses me (AND KISSES ME!) and *trring!* I turn into a man and everything fits into place.

But it's not going to happen like that, is it?

I can see it now. I'll just get old, gasping with ambition, and then I'll choke on my own vomit when I'm seventy – after a confused night's boozing, after having tried to seduce my daughter-in-law over the dinner table. (And somehow I get the feeling I'll be more than willing to call it a day, that I'll be packed and ready to go.)

But we're not considering that right now, are we?

We are now a man. We are now *action* man.

Hand me that bomb Mike. Thanks buddy.

Ray is definitely not action man. I know when he's arrived because I hear his car revving up as he parks on the footpath. Before he stops he puts his foot on the accelerator and revs up the engine. Even that sounds like it's in slow motion. It takes him hours to get out of the car. He picks up his bag and tidies the front seat cushion and sits there looking at the floor mats before he finally gets out and comes to the door. He wears little-old-man clothes as well: antiquated metal arm-bands and leather shoes. Ray the jazz keyboardist.

I like him because he doesn't want anything: he just does what I want and then he leaves. His car drops off the footpath and he'll remember to indicate too late; most days there'll be sniper fire from the rear as he's gunned down by passing motorists.

Dee has gone to Bangkok. I see her in some dim back room with a beaded curtain, finally satiated, finally at that place where we all want to be. The struggle is over for Dee.

Actually I'm pleased she's gone, she was getting on my nerves.

Ray and I went out for coffee today. I did my usual trick of wearing something of Tracey's and leaving it behind. I've nearly got through everything of hers. I hate putting her things on, no matter how many comments of wonderfulness they're capable of engendering. I take them off as soon as I can, and leave them behind, pretending I've forgotten them. I left something at Hilary Hancock's – a little cardigan which I left on the couch. Sometimes people will run after me, *you forgot this!* and I'll play along, thanking them.

Nobody noticed the jacket I left at the coffee shop – when we left I could see it through the window, still sitting on the back of the chair.

Ray eats slowly and his hands tremble. I told him about Tracey's mother, the whole story: what happened at the wedding (in full nipplistic detail), and how she turned up at our place a couple of nights later. (I didn't tell him about me reeling outside and wetting my pants as I squatted in the garden; how I couldn't get my tights down, and how I lay in the foetal position under a bush for an hour before ending up in the back seat of the car battered in vomit and urine and bark chips, where Tracey found me.)

Ray took it all in like a brain-damaged maths teacher, hanging his head and eating his scone while he listened, and then, quite uncharacteristically I thought, he laughed, and scone and jam and butter came spitting across the table at me.

James was in a Monday night nihilistic funk, thinking about hiring a male prostitute, but he didn't have enough money. I'd told him about Tracey's mother and then instantly regretted it. Tracey was having a shower and when she came out she made some comment about having no tits and James said, *pity you didn't get any of your mother's, love,* and then cackled like the fucking homo he was. I could have killed the fuck. I got him in the kitchen later and he did his usual back-pedalling gayboy number and pretended he was about to wash the dishes. He left the sink half full of water and went and got the latest *Boys Like Us* from his room, and sat on the couch reading the Boys Wanted column out loud.

Tracey was egging him on, sitting on the floor cutting things out of magazines – pictures of babies and fuck knows what else. She was making a birthday card for one of her friends. (The telephone hadn't stopped ringing since she'd moved in, and they all seemed to know me: *Hi, it's Katherine, is Tracey home? Hello Ruth. Is Tracey there?*)

I was trying to watch TV. I didn't feel that well actually. Liz had just rung and asked if I would go into work and turn the coffee machine off. I told her I couldn't drive because of my hand, and she hung up on me. I was on the verge of asking Tracey if she would take me to a doctor – James would be useless; he'd probably want to masturbate in the car on the way – when the phone rang again. I thought it might be Liz ringing back, but it was Maxine. For Tracey. Tracey trundled over to the phone, snapping the scissors at James, as if it were perfectly normal that Maxine should be calling her.

While she was on the phone, the door bell rang and James went to get it. He returned with *Faye* behind him, dressed in an ethnic jumper and leggings, with white sports socks bunched around the ankles. She looked like a potter. Of horrible things. Tracey covered the phone with her hand and said, "*What are you doing here?*"

"I rang, but it was engaged," she said, looking at James.

I thought I might have a fit of some sort, so deep was my discomfiture, so red was my blush, so profound was my shame. *What was she doing here?* It was an awful invasion. It was the *worst possible* invasion. The flat was a tip (not that that mattered because I didn't care about her) and, worse, I was sober. I did something I hadn't done since I was eight and my father inadvertently lifted me up in the air and revealed to the party-goers below that I wasn't wearing any pants under my nightie – *I ran from the room.* Staggered, jogged, rushed: whatever. I got the fuck out of there as fast as I could. Tracey came into the bedroom a few minutes later.

"What's going on?"

"Sorry," I said, "I don't feel like visitors."

"I didn't know she was coming. Will you come and help me?"

"She's your mother. I don't need to see her."

Tracey stood there looking at me glumly.

"*OK*, I'll come out in a minute."

I left it for ten and then stepped boldly into the lounge.

Faye was sitting at the table drinking gin. She looked at me cautiously, like a dog seeing its new owner approaching. If she had a tail she might have wagged it once or twice.

"Sore hand." I said, holding it up and grimacing. "How are you?"

"Oh? Yes, I –"

"Why don't you just say *good?* Why do you have to make everything such a *drama?*" Tracey said. "Ruth only asked *how you were.*"

"Oh. Yes. Good," Faye said to the couch, used to being booted in the ribs by her daughter. She had another mouthful of gin before getting up to go to the toilet, knocking some magazines off the table as she went. Tracey carried on cutting out her pictures, helped out by her tongue on the tight corners.

I could feel her mother's eyes on me as she came back into the room. Fuck off. Fuck off! It wasn't me. I did not suck your tits. I did not. I did not.

Jesus they were huge. It was a wonder I didn't suffocate in there.

"So, Ruth…" she said, sitting down, "how are you?" Magazines cascading to the floor again.

"*Oh for God's sake!*" (Tracey.)

"Would you like another gin?" I asked, just as James came into the room. "James, will you get it?" James looked a bit pissed off that his gin was being pillaged, but took her glass anyway.

"Do you have your friends over, Tracey?"

Tracey hacked at a magazine.

"No."

"Oh? Who was that driving off?"

"No one. *Who?*"

"He was much too old for you anyway," her mother said, looking at me and winking.

"What did he look like?" Tracey sighed.

"Well…" she said, enjoying herself, "he had white hair –"

White hair? Who the fuck was that? I jumped up and went over to the window, startling Tracey's mother, only remembering when I got there that you couldn't see the road from that window. I dropped the curtain and went into the kitchen and stood there. James was chopping up a lemon. Back into the lounge. Tracey's mother was looking at me with maternal concern combined with a splash of longing. Everything was tightening up. My chest, my arms: there were pins and needles in my arms.

"Excuse me," I said. "Ah, yeah."

Into the bathroom. Too bright. Into the bedroom. Turn on the light. Standing at the mirror pulling at the neck of my jersey. My arms were seizing up. I was having a stroke. I was having a stroke. Back into the lounge.

"I'm having a stroke."

Tracey laughed.

"I fucking am. Call an ambulance."

Tracey looked at my arms, which were outstretched stiffly in front of me, then all the alarm bells went off. She dialled an ambulance and Faye led me over to the table where I sat in the chair, my mouth skewing into stroke position. James got his pipe off the mantelpiece and ran around looking for any other evidence of illegal activity before the authorities arrived. For some reason they turned all the lights on and the TV off. I sat there in the dazzling light having a stroke.

Please come, please come, please come before I die in this chair in this shithole.

All that promise all those years ago: I'm riding my bike fast, the sun is warm on my face and I know every pothole, every house, and

I'm listing what I want: I want to be Miss World, I want to take my parents on a round-the-world trip, I want to be seventeen, I want to have a horse; and then the world turns some more, so slowly I hardly felt it, so quickly there's bile in my throat, and... time's up Ruth. Thank you.

We all heard the ambulance siren. Tracey was waiting by the front door and yelled *They're here!* and shortly afterwards two ambulance women sauntered into the lounge.

"Hello," one said, looking around the room with a frightening lack of concern as she took off her gloves. "What can we do for you?"

"I'm having a stroke," I squeezed out of the corner of my mouth, my body jerking in the chair like a caricature of a lunatic.

The other one came over to me.

"Hello," she said. "You're having a stroke?"

"Yeah."

"What's your name?"

Faye and Tracey both said, *Ruth.*

"Hello Ruth... Mmm. Move your hand for me. Right. OK. This is the worse case of hyperventilation I've seen." She knelt beside me, "Mo?"

Mo, who had been looking at Tracey's handiwork on the floor with a bemused smile, came over.

"Look how the hand has gone like that. What's wrong with your other hand? I'm Sally, by the way. Can someone make Ruth a cup of tea please?"

Faye puffed towards the door asking everyone how they had it. Tracey stood behind me stroking my hair, and in the background James got ready to go out, stealthily filling his pockets with keys and condoms and amyl, off to scour the streets for any early evening signs of desperation. Sally took the bandage off my hand.

"That's a mess. You'll need to go to the hospital for that. What's happened is that you're hyperventilating Ruth. You've been breathing rapidly and taken in more oxygen than you need and that's washed out too much carbon dioxide from your lungs. That's all. Have a cup of tea now and then I think you should have that hand seen to at the hospital. Have you been under any stress lately?" She looked up at Tracey.

"No," Tracey said. "I don't think so."

"I have," I said. "Yeah."

"You'll be all right," Sally said, holding my fingers. "Nothing serious."

Faye came in with the tea.

"I've put sugar in it," she said handing it to me.

"Thanks." I couldn't hold the cup properly and hot tea spilt on my trousers. Tracey and Faye both went to wipe at it, Faye getting there first. The two ambulance women gulped their tea and gave me further instructions on what to do if it happened again, and then left. Faye let them out, pleased to have something valid to do.

I put my cup on the table and sat there shocked. Jesus Christ. What next? I went to get up. "Sorry," I said.

"Oh –" Faye said, touching my arm. "Do you think you should be standing up?"

"Yeah, I think I should lie down for a while."

"You have to go to the hospital," Tracey said.

"I'll do the dishes, shall I?" Faye volunteered.

"*No.* I'll call you a taxi."

"I don't mind coming with you –"

"I'm going to lie down," I said, and sat on the couch. The phone rang. Tracey got it. It was someone she knew because she gurgled away and laughed and then said, *Ruth hyperventilated and the ambulance came.* I gave her the filthiest look I could muster and mouthed *Who is it?*

She has to breathe into a paper bag next time, she said, looking at me with delight. *It's Martin*, she mouthed back.

I reached out for the phone and she brought it over, grinning away.

"It's Martin. What's been happening?"

"Don't listen to her. Nothing."

No, I am not crabbed on the couch in post-traumatic hyperventilation shock. I'm engrossed in one of my many hobbies. You're who?

"I rang to see if you wanted to come to dinner."

Images of kissing and spaghetti.

"To dinner?"

"Yep. On Saturday night."

"That would be really nice," I crooned, and saw the mother/daughter combo looking at me keenly.

"What do you and Tracey eat?"

Tracey?

"Whatever."

"Excellent."

"What brought this on?" I said.

He laughed (the nervous one). "Come round whenever you like."

"OK." (Girlfriend, love object of Martin Myers, slightly bored now.)

He lowered his voice and said jokingly, "Look forward to it."

I handed the phone back to Tracey.

"What did he want?" she said.

I didn't have to tell her. I could always tell him she couldn't make it.

"He invited us to dinner on Saturday night."

"Me as well?"

"I imagine it's *you* he wants to see," I said, putting my feet up on the couch and holding the cushion to my chest. "It's cold in here."

"I don't think it's *me*," she said, but we both knew it was. We both knew that *very well indeed.*

"Who's that?" Tracey's mother asked, trying to turn the heater up.

"*I'll do that,*" Tracey said. "No one. A friend of Ruth's. God – *hyperventilating.*"

"Yeah," I said, fucked off with her.

I wanted to go and lie on the bed, but Tracey insisted that I lie on the couch and went and got the duvet. "I'll get changed and take you to the hospital," she said when she came back, "and phone a taxi," she said to her mother.

I dug myself deep into the duvet, hoping the taxi would come quickly. Then I suddenly remembered the cause of all this. My heart hit my ribs.

I poked my head up. "Faye?"

Faye was sitting at the table trying to read the cover of a magazine which was the wrong way up.

"That man you saw outside? Was he a hippy?"

"A hippy?" A car horn tooted. "No. I don't think so. Ruth, I –"

"Don't worry about it. You better go."

Tracey came into the room, newly lipsticked. "The cab's here," she said to her mother and headed down the hall, expecting her to follow.

"Bobbye," I said to Faye, unable to look at her.

Faye stood up and shuffled sideways through the door, and then made a funny grunting noise.

"Sorry," I said, meaning it.

She stopped and backed up slightly and then turned, filling the doorway.

"*Faye!*" Tracey screamed.

"You'd better go," I said.

"I'm caught on the door."

The taxi tooted again.

"*Hurry up!*"

Faye pulled her jersey free, her eyes swivelling back to the couch. "Well, I hope you're feeling better," she said. Linger. Pause.

"Thanks."

And slowly, belabouredly, down the hall with her, she was gone.

I lay back on the couch, awash with everything. The throbbing in my hand reminded me I had to go to the hospital. I felt relief that I hadn't had a stroke, but I also felt scared.

"Do you think that the Prozac might have caused that?" I asked Tracey when she came back in.

"No. *God*. My *mother*."

"She's all right," I said. "I thought I was having a stroke."

"I *know*," she said, excited, "I thought you were having one too!"

We conveniently omitted any more talk of her mother, or Martin's phone call, and got ourselves out to the car.

"Never a dull moment anyway," Tracey said as she started the car. "What was that about a man outside?"

"What?" I said, immediately trying to think of something plausible to tell her, although why I should lie to her, I don't know. I wanted to tell her, but in order for it to make any sense I'd have to tell her the full story. Hedgehog and all. Maybe I could. *Could I?*

"I think I'm going mad," I said, and chuckled to soften the blow, mainly to myself.

She looked across at me.

"Watch the road."

"You think you're going mad? Why?"

"I don't know. I think I've been having hallucinations or something – well, I thought I had, but then – when your mother said –"

"Who do you think you've been seeing? That man?"

"You know!"

"No I don't. Tell me."

"Maxine fucking told you!"

"No she didn't. Well, she did but –"

"When were you talking to Maxine?"

"I talk to her all the time. She calls me from work."

"Does she?"

"What's the big deal?"

"No. No big deal."

I sat there glowering out the window at the dark.

"I think you and I should just call it a day," I said.

"*Ruth!*"

"Well I do. We've got nothing in common –"

"*Yes we have –*"

"It's not working out. I made a mistake."

"*You* made a mistake? Thanks for telling me," she said angrily.

"Well, you know –"

"*I've just moved in.*"

"Yeah well –"

She drove in silence until we pulled into the hospital, then as we hurtled around the roundabout she said, "I *am* what you want."

I looked at her profile. She certainly looked like what I wanted; if she dyed her hair and got some green coloured contacts and became a different person she'd be even better. But that was beside the point: what I really wanted was Martin Myers, and that wasn't about to happen with her in the frame.

"I think I'd be better off by myself," I said as we got out of the car.

"Well, too bad. You're not going to be," she said, taking my arm and leading me into the hospital.

Two nurses looked at us with interest. Despite the circumstances I felt the usual cheap thrill.

"Stop worrying about me running off with Martin. Honestly, I don't fancy him," she said, holding my arm tightly. "I fancy *you.*"

"Do you?" I said grumpily, secretly pleased that she wasn't thinking of running off with Martin.

"Can I help you two girls?" the woman at admissions asked.

Tracey ignored her and kissed me on the cheek. "*Yes*. Silly."

"Can I help you?"

"Sorry," I smiled at the woman, feeling more of a bond with Tracey than I had since I'd met her. I held onto Tracey's arm while I gave the woman my details, and then Tracey and I sat together on the plastic seats. Tracey held my hand.

"See," she said, using her eyes to maximum effect on me. "*See?*"

And I did. For a moment there at the hospital I really thought I did.

I had to take a course of antibiotics and was *very lucky girl* not to have septicaemia. Tracey called me *darling* in front of the doctor, a little Indian man who buzzed in and buzzed out, but I couldn't work out whether the look on his face was one of distaste or boredom. I'd mentioned hyperventilating to him and he acted as if he hadn't heard me and continued to write out the prescription. *Yes?* he said, when he'd finished, *What do you want to know?* I didn't know what it was I wanted to know, so I just said *nothing* and changed the subject.

There was something about Indian men I didn't like, something intimidating, even though physically they weren't. I loved Indian women though: all smudgy blacks and browns, and those swirls of colour, those wrappings of green and gold and red and yellow! Poor Indian women – having to be married to Indian men. Why wasn't everybody bisexual? Life would be so much simpler!

Tracey and I were laughing about this next morning (and as we did, another strand came undone: why didn't Tracey correct me and say *gay?* Why wasn't everybody *gay*, Ruth?). We were in my room, both on a bit of a post-hospital high, and Tracey was going through my wardrobe looking at my clothes while I sat up in bed with a cup of tea: my clean, newly bandaged hand a symbol of healing. At least, it seemed so. Polly was asleep on the end of the bed.

I'd taken the day off work: Tracey had called Maxine for me and then gone out to buy the paper to see if there were any jobs in it for her. There wasn't anything going in film or TV: she was going to have to start ringing places to see if they needed anyone. I said I'd help: we'd look up production houses and compile a list of addresses. She also wanted to get some photos done to send to model agencies.

I looked at her while I drank my tea, thinking how dishonest I was with her, how I related to her on the most superficial level, and how she had no idea I was doing it. And even if I'd told her, I'm sure she wouldn't have believed me. The me she saw was a different one than the *me* me. I related to her in the same way that I did with my mother – I kept things from her. My mother used to call it *lying by omission*. Apparently I was the master of it. I expect I was, but if that was the case then I was fucking sure it had something to do with *her*. Bound to have. I couldn't remember. Memory by omission.

And then there was Tracey's mother. Maybe I'd sucked Faye's tits because I wanted to suck my own mother's tits? It was true I hadn't been breast-fed, but, oh dear God please *no*.

"Why do you think women are attracted to women?" I asked Tracey.

"I don't know. Do you think I should have my hair cut for the photos?"

"It looks good. Your mother likes it anyway," I said and laughed, trying to wedge Faye into the conversation.

"My *mother?*"

"Why don't you like her? What's wrong with her?"

"I hate her. Can I borrow this black dress?"

"That's not very rational is it? There must be a reason why you hate her. Is it because she's fat?"

"*No.*"

"Why then?"

"I don't want to talk about it. Why do you want to know anyway?"

The opportunity presented itself, so I lied.

"Because I want to know more about you."

(Fuck, that sounded false. She must have seen through that.)

"*Do you?*" She came over to the bed and lay across me, propping herself up on one elbow and looking at me theatrically, "I'll need a joint if I'm going to tell you."

She was very pretty. I could see why she was so popular.

"OK. Go and get one. Better get our Prozac too. Oh, and the antibiotics!" We both laughed and she lifted the sleeping Polly up by the back legs, turned her in midair and kissed her, before depositing her under the sheet next to my hip and sashaying out the door. Polly struggled free and looked at me warily before jumping to the floor and toddling out the door after her.

Being in my room was like being inside an orange iceblock. When the curtains were closed and the sun was shining, the whole room was a lovely bright orange. It looked different now that Tracey had moved in, more homely.

"Why don't you wear my black polo neck?" I started to say when she came back in. "It's –"

"Yuk. I *hate* polo necks!"

"I wear them –"

"I know. They're awful."

"Thanks –"

"It's nothing to do with *you*. I don't like them on me. Here, here're your pills."

The spell was broken. Tracey the competitor was back. Tracey the predator was home. Tracey the polo-neck hater who lived in my room, had returned.

"I'm getting up," I said.

"OK," she said, going back to the wardrobe. "What day will we do my photos?"

"I don't know."

"What's the matter?"

"Nothing."

"Alicia likes this red. She's got a dress this colour."

"Really?"

The back of her head moved imperceptibly, but she didn't turn around.

Why aren't you what I want? Why can I never get what I want?

I am a vampire Tracey. Can you imagine that pain? Would it be so painful: that you couldn't bear it? Oh sweet Jesus. I'm swelling like a tick. But over the wanting, Tracey, not you.

(But right now I'm going to run to the toilet and lock myself in again. And I want you to leave me alone while I pace like a caged polar bear between the toilet and the shower. And I want you to be gone when I come out. (Were you ever there? When I come back into the room, when I look back in... a year? Can it have been a year already?

Two years later? Were you real?)

The truth is, whatever your name is, whoever you are, I want to run further than the toilet: *I want to run home.* I want to run and run until I get to the big walnut tree on the lawn, near the croquet pitch and the old apple tree, beneath which my slender mother sits, one arm swinging languorously in the storybook warmth of home. And look! There's my father in a clean white shirt, happy and successful, smoking, by the tennis courts.)

15: All blood and bone and brown velvet

Tracey chose a long salmon-pink gown with covered buttons, and gold high heels to wear to Martin's. Not wishing to be outdone, although this was inevitable, I also wore a gown – one of hers, a brown velvet one with a satin ribbon that tied at the back. My own footwear was somewhat more prosaic: brown pointy boots, also Tracey's. We sprayed perfume everywhere and went for maximum eyeliner. I wore red lipstick and she wore pink. She looked gorgeous. She told me I looked gorgeous. I felt *reasonably* gorgeous, then more gorgeous after two glasses of wine.

I'd decided to take the rest of the week off. Liz had rung for a daily progress report: her voice becoming more strangled and less compassionate as Thursday became Friday. She even tried to convince me to come in for a few hours on Saturday. I'd said I couldn't, and even if I could it would be too difficult to work with one hand – I could barely hold a cup of coffee, let alone start typing anything.

Which wasn't strictly true – the antibiotics had worked, and my hand was feeling a lot better so I'd started doing some knitting. I was making a jumper for Martin. A black one with a crew neck. Pure wool. Knitting was therapeutic, or I'd been told it was. I'd had some sort of nervous breakdown when I was twenty and I remember somebody suggesting I take up knitting. I didn't just take up knitting – I went out and found the most complicated Fair Aisle pattern ever seen on the face of the earth, with at least six different colours through it, and then spent months, in between crying, trying to knit a hideous waistcoat which ended up under the bed for a decade, whereupon I took it out and finished it, only realising when I sewed it up that it was such a bizarre shape it would only fit a very tall ten-year-old. I was going to have it framed as a testimony to perseverance, but then I couldn't decide if it was perseverance or non-performance I'd be saluting.

When Tracey saw what I was doing she got all excited and went out and bought her own needles and started doing the front while I did the back. Her knitting was looser than mine and she dropped stitches and left big holes at the front of rows. It had a certain charm I suppose.

I didn't want her helping – I wanted to do my own knitting – but Tracey, as I was beginning to discover, was adept at muscling in on any activity that had a payoff.

There'd been no sign of any recurring hyperventilation. More a pervading air of anxiety. I'd begun to project disaster everywhere. For example: as I put the ball gown on I imagined my heel getting caught in the hem of it and tearing it; while I poured the wine I had a vision of smashing the glass against the table and pushing the edge into Tracey's face, uncontrollably; as we went to the car I saw myself run into the road and flip off a passing car bonnet. While I was in the toilet I imagined one of those big ball things that they knock buildings down with smashing through the side of the house and pulverising me against the toilet wall.

And all this in the space of an hour or two.

I was also more than a little perturbed by the notion that the guy in the tracksuit might actually be real, and not just some drug-induced phantasm. Who was he? Where had I seen him before? (He was in there somewhere, buried deep in there, in my subconscious, like a character in a particularly complex dream that you can't quite put your finger on.) Round and round it went. Just who had Faye seen outside? Was it him? Who was he? I wanted to ring Faye and quiz her but I couldn't face having to talk to her again.

I felt like I was caught in a kind of twilight zone between reality and whatever the opposite is. And just what exactly did they put in acid these days? I kept having visions of some smelly moron in a basement with a collection of rusty drums and an eyedropper, not touching the shit himself.

But alcohol is a wonderful thing: it gets you in a ball gown from the house to the car, borrowed brown pointy boots and all, then it arranges your coat for you, and even passes you your purse. (It only gets pissed off with you later on – and by then it's sick to bloody death of you – but at the start it's optimistic, really helpful.)

As usual Tracey had no money so I gave her some to buy a bottle of wine to take with us. She double-parked outside the wine shop and ran in. The shop was one of those upmarket ones with expensive spot lighting and neons, and people were hurrying in and out. Tracey landed in a tangle of feathers and squawking in the doorway and everyone looked up. It was obvious they thought she was someone famous. I could feel the effect she was having from the car. The man behind the counter watched her every move, briskly serving distracted customers who were also trying to get a look at her.

I sat in the car trying to hide from the tooting and shaking fists and so forth being directed towards me as cars banked up behind us. I was going to get out and go round to the driver's side and try and find a parking space, but I didn't want to get out of the car dressed like I was. Why had I worn a fucking ball gown? Only thirteen-year-olds dressed the same way. Tracey looked UTTERLY BRILLIANT in a ball gown: her pink was the pink of princesses; my brown the brown of, well, brown. My brown, of course, would look like the brown of Belgian chocolates on Tracey, the brown of freshly turned earth on a spring morning, on Tracey.

"I don't think I should have worn this dress," I said as she got back in the car – but she didn't hear me: she was too busy mouthing *sorry* and smiling at a car full of sly-looking men who'd slowed down to check her out.

She laughed happily and turned to me, "Sorry?"

"This dress. I feel silly in it."

"No, you look lovely," she said. "It suits you."

"Yours looks better –"

"No it doesn't – What? You want to wear this one?"

"No –"

"OK, we'll go home and you can wear this. I'll wear that," she said, her foot slipping off the accelerator, pitching us both towards the windscreen.

"No! No! Don't be silly. Just drive to Martin's."

She looked relieved and changed into second. "*Now*," she smiled, full beam, "which way?"

"Hi-eeee."

Martin looked at our dresses and laughed.

"Thank you," Tracey said and did a twirl. The pleasure on her face was pure and childlike; her eyes gleamed, and Martin and I had to duck to avoid being sprinkled with the fairy dust spinning off her shoulders. I wanted to pinch her.

(This thought must have been transferred to her because she looked at me guiltily – and so quickly that Martin didn't notice, and I doubt whether she was aware that I had registered it either.)

"We look wonderful, don't we?" she said, and stepped back magnanimously to include me.

"You do," he said, and leapt up the stairs in front of us. He stopped at the top and held the door open. There was a man sitting in the lounge drinking beer. He was good-looking in a springy-haired big-nosed sort of way. He stood up as we came in.

"Nigel," Martin said. We all shook hands and Martin went to the kitchen to get some wine glasses. Tracey immediately sat down on the couch next to Nigel while I pulled a chair over from the table.

"Yep," Nigel said, putting his hand behind his head and smoothing his hair. He shifted around on the couch to get a better look at Tracey.

"Are you a friend of Martin's?" Tracey asked.

"I'm his boss."

"*Are* you?" She laughed and sat forward, crossing her hands over one knee.

He finished his beer. "What about you?" he said, crushing the can and putting it on the floor.

"I've just finished a media studies degree."

Liar. That was the second time she'd done that. Nigel looked impressed.

"I'm looking for a job at the moment," Tracey said. "Ruth's in PR."

"Is that right?" He burped and looked at my tits.

Martin came in with the glasses. He was wearing a faded orange shirt and black trousers, with bare feet. Even if he wasn't your type you couldn't help but think he was attractive. He had something of the pirate about him, something fluid and Fuck it, I was making it too obvious. Not only was I dressing like a thirteen-year-old, I was beginning to think like one as well. I turned to Nigel, annoyed with myself.

"Your company's got a strange name hasn't it?" I knew what it was – *Producers/Directors* – it wasn't that strange. I'd seen it in an article in *AdHoc*, What's in a Name?, which included a photo of *rising star, Martin Myers, on location with Fuji.*

"Yup," he said, not telling me. He sat up off the couch and pulled at his trouser legs.

"I work for Liz Bailey," I said.

"Uh-huh. When's this dinner happening then, Marty?" he said, and reached for the remote control. "You haven't got a copy of the Cleopatra vid have you mate?"

"Yeah, yeah. You want to see it again?" Martin said, opening the wine.

"Yeah. Whack it in. We've got another one coming up for them."

"Excellent. Olive?" Martin said and handed out the olives before putting a video in the machine. Nigel suddenly became all business, leaning forward and burping and watching the screen intently. Martin stopped what he was doing and stood there motionless while Cleopatra ordered a group of handmaidens from the room, and a snake slithered under the bath. A black panther watched from the shadows, eyes burning into hers. It snarled and as it leapt forward it morphed into a black man wearing cycling shorts and carrying a jewelled box. Cleopatra growled and ran her fingernails over the man's glistening torso before taking the box from him, slowly opening it to reveal an icecream shaped like a pyramid. She lay back and closed her eyes, and as the icecream touched her lips a sultry male voice said: *New Pyramid. It's everything you'll ever. Want.*

"Excellent," Nigel said when it had finished.

"That's really great," Tracey said, uncrossing her legs and looking admiringly at Martin. There followed a round of back-slapping with Tracey playing secretary to the stars, and Nigel eyeing her up while he sank another beer and half-listened to Martin arguing the case for a bigger computer animation budget.

In theory, Martin was addressing Nigel, but he was trying to *convince* Tracey – of his desirability, judging by the amount of eyebrow jumping and general enthusiasm that was being generated. He never talked to me like that – all my exchanges with him were laconic, strangled affairs. I sat there sipping my wine, feeling left out. Eventually they got round to me. Or Tracey did. I saw the words coming out of her mouth before I heard them. She was going to ask me what I thought of it.

"It was OK," I said.

Nobody said anything.

A year ago I would have been PR'ing for Africa – but it wasn't a year ago, it was now and Martin fancied Tracey. And she fucking fancied him! It was fucking obvious. They kept looking at each other all the time.

"What do you want me to say?"

"Say what you think," Nigel challenged.

Ho-hum.

"OK. I thought it was crap if you really want to know."

Nigel laughed uncomfortably. "We don't write them love," he said, and topped up everybody's wine. That was me off the Christmas card list. Fuck him. Wanker.

Tracey, meanwhile, set about making amends for me by cheerfully setting the table, looking around for something to use as a centre-piece, while I sat subtly ostracised on the chair. She balanced two video tapes on the table and curtsied. Martin laughed. She then found some candles on the shelf and lit them. Nigel and Martin went into the kitchen and after they'd gone Tracey turned the light off to see what the effect of the candlelight was.

"I'm *so* hungry," she said, looking through the CDs. "Are you?"

"No. Not really. I'm surprised you're hungry."

"I know!" she said. "Me too!" Tracey was always delighted to discover something new about herself.

"What's that?" Martin said, coming in with a tureen.

"Ruth's not hungry. Prozac. Yum, that looks nice. What is it?"

"Soup," Martin said, putting it on the table and looking at me briefly before heading back to the kitchen.

"I didn't want him to know that."

"Sorry."

"*You're* on it anyway. Why do you have to tell everybody everything?"

"I *don't*."

"Yes you do."

"I didn't realise it was a secret."

Shaping up to be a fine evening all round. I could feel the first brush of drunkenness sidle up to me as I stood up. I concentrated on standing up straight. These boots made you feel incredibly tall. More wine. What the fuck. I went into the toilet and sat there looking at the door. It wasn't fair. Martin might not be interested in me, but Tracey wasn't going to have him. Some thrashy guitar music came on. Now Tracey would be able to slip into the conversation how she played bass. In a band.

Yeah.

Never underestimate the cuntiness of women. New motto. Better go to the toilet as well.

I managed to pee on the bottom of my dress somehow, but you

couldn't see the wet patch unless you were looking.

They were all in the kitchen when I came out: Tracey and Nigel were watching Martin cut up some garlic bread.

"Can I do anything?" I asked cheerfully.

"It's done," Martin said, passing the plate to Tracey.

They started to go through to the lounge. "Are you coming, Ruth?" Tracey said. "Hey. What's that on your dress?"

"Nothing. I'm just getting some wine." I waited until they were gone and then filled my glass before opening the back door on to the balcony. I took off the boots and climbed down the fire escape stairs and perched on the bottom rung. I used to do this sort of thing when I was a kid, and now I remembered why I'd stopped doing it. It was cold and dark.

They'd all be sitting at the table waiting for me now.

I sat there for a full fifteen minutes bunched over, scraping at the dirt with a twig, waiting for someone to come and get me. The cold put its skinny little arms around me and I shivered. *Bastards. They'd started without me.* I'd better get back. I was just deciding what to do next when the door opened and Tracey looked over the balcony rail.

"Ruth? What are you doing?"

"Nothing. Go away."

"*Oh, stay there if you want to,*" she said, and went inside, slamming the door.

Fucking cow. I made it up the steps in record time, ripping her dress on a piece of metal as I went. She was in the kitchen waiting for me.

"Come out here," I said.

"*What?*"

"I can't believe you let me do that. Sit down there for all that time –"

"*What?* You went down there. What was I supposed to do?"

"You could have come and got me –"

"You're mad –"

"What did you call me?"

"You're – you're a *spinner!*"

"A *spinner?*" I said. "*You're* the one who's a spinner. Where are you going?"

"I'm going inside."

"Fuck you."

"Fuck you too."

"No thanks. And while you're fucking Martin you can tell him he's a cunt from me."

"*What?*" She stopped and came back out. "*What* did you say?"

"You heard me. You and Martin. Why don't you just fuck each other and get it over with?"

"I'm not having this conversation."

"Yes you are."

"No I'm not," she said and shut the door in my face. I heard her walking off. I banged on the door and she came back and opened it.

"Thank you." I left her boots where they were and pushed past her and out the front door, then remembered my purse was in the lounge with the car keys in it.

Nigel was standing by the bookshelf looking at his mobile phone, and Martin was sitting at the table smoking, seemingly unconcerned, although I could sense an element of fear in there somewhere.

I picked up my bag.

"Enjoy your soup?" I said.

"Yes thank you," said Nigel, still studying his phone.

Martin just looked at me.

"Cheerio then."

"Bye," they chorused.

"Oh yeah," I said, hitching up my pantaloons and tumbling down the side of the monkey bars, "and that *Nu Car* ad was crap as well."

Nigel burped. Martin looked at me contemptuously and stubbed out his cigarette, and Tracey followed me to the front door, which I slammed in her face.

"By-eeee," I yelled, and strained to hear a reply as I stomped down the stairs in my stockinged feet. None appeared to be forthcoming.

I'd blown it again. What did I do that for? Jesus. Now I had to drive home in this fucking dress – which I did, my trembling lips giving way to crying before I'd turned the corner of the street. Fucking Prozac. It wasn't helping. Nothing was helping. I was fucking mental. Fucking *mental*.

(fucking mental to leave her there WITH HIM)

I heard James's CD player as soon as I got out of the car. The cat was asleep on a pile of Tracey's clothes in the hall. The light was off in the lounge but the door was open and I could see a Japanese boy of about fifteen sitting on the couch dressed in his underpants drinking gin, his eyes bulging at something. I couldn't see James but I assumed he was in there as well. It didn't take much imagination to work out what he was doing. I walked down the hall to my bedroom.

My room smelt mouldy, and the cat box behind the door had runny puddles of shit sitting on it. It was only quarter past ten. James was probably going to a club. I decided I'd go with him and stay out as late as possible. Better than sitting around waiting for Tracey to come home.

I found my packet of Prozac and took ten pills and placed them in a little pile on the bed and then went down the hall to the kitchen. The Japanese boy and James had gone into James's bedroom. I got a tin of sardines out of the cupboard and opened it, and waved it under Polly's sleeping nose on the way back to my room. She stirred and then slipped off her temporary bed and followed me, miaowing as I made up ten tiny fish balls and fed them to her one by one. She didn't even blink, she ate them happily, sniffing around for more when she'd finished. I put the tin on the floor for her, and went to the bathroom to wash my hands.

James and his friend were back in the lounge, kneeling by the coffee table. I went in and turned the music down and James nearly choked on his gin when he saw me. "When did you come in?" he said, feeling around the front of his trousers.

"Before."

"Where's Tracey?" He got to his feet, suddenly looking scandalised. "*Is Martin Myers here?*"

The Japanese boy looked at me excitedly.

"No. Don't ask. And who are you?" I asked the boy, who panicked and looked at James. He was clearly disturbed enough without having to answer questions of this nature.

James carried on sorting out his drugs. Obviously he didn't know either.

I drank a couple of gins while they got themselves ready. We smoked a joint in the car on the way to the club and drove around the streets skulling the rest of the gin before rolling up to the club around midnight. The Japanese boy was on another planet, eyes heavenward as he hopscotched around in the dance-floor lights. James disappeared as soon as we got there, leaving me alone in the beer-stained shadows. I still had Tracey's brown frock on but I couldn't have cared less: the preceding events had left me feeling somewhat disturbed myself, but I was drunk enough for it to have changed shape.

I sank onto the floor up against the wall, shadowy shapes of men in groups shifting and distorting above me. The eternal teenager, doomed to be stuck in a perverse adolescent mood, my faults sat like thick pudding in my head; they pervaded my being. *To sleep, perchance to dream*, became a schoolgirl mantra; it rolled around in my head as the gayboys came and went. And then I wanted a razorblade. In my drunken state the thought of cutting my arms seemed appealing. Not for any big statement, nor a suicide bid – just a bit of good old forearm chopping. If I hadn't been so drunk I would have thought it was unspeakably stupid – but as usual the alcohol changed the shape of things. Time flitted past, chirping and twittering like birds, and I remember I talked to people. I borrowed some money off James, and I think I even had a dance. All the while I was smiling, I didn't want any of them to know. I bought a gin and tonic and smashed the glass in the toilet sink when no one was in there, and hiding a piece of glass in my hand – from whom I don't know because no one was paying the slightest bit of attention to me – I went back to my corner and slid down into it, and set about cutting up my arm. I cut it five or six times: went in as deep as I could; weird, weird. Shaking heart; grateful pain, fucking outrageous. Christ. *Christ.* I rolled my sleeve down again. And then I can't remember. Like so many nights I can't remember the rest, although I know I didn't pass out: I must have stayed there doing fuck knows what until I got a taxi home. I had a receipt in my bag the next day. A fucking receipt. *Drop me off here thanks driver. Oh, and could I have a receipt please?*

I woke up in the middle of a panic attack. Heart pounding, head caving in. Where was I? Home. I was home. What – ? Jesus fuck. I didn't – *please* say I didn't. I turned on the light and looked at my arm. Oh my god. Where's Tracey? Not here. Not here. She's not *fucking home*. WHERE THE FUCK IS SHE THEN?

"When was this?" Ray said, looking up from the kitchen table. He'd been sitting there reading a page he'd picked up off the floor. I didn't see what he was doing until it was too late.

"What bit are you reading?" I said, getting up and standing behind him.

(Please don't let him have the page about him and me having sex, or the cat, or the last bit for that matter.)

"Ah..." he ran his hand through his thinning hair.

A page from the beginning. The homesick feeling.

"I'm not using that. It's not true anyway."

He turned the page over and stared at the back of it which was blank.

"Where's it set?"

"… I don't think I say…"

He put it down on the table. "Is it a novel?"

"Sort of."

"It's doomy."

"It's what?"

"Doomy."

"Oh."

I suppose it is. Doomy. I wanted to point my tight little face in Ray's direction and say *I don't expect everybody's story ends with a gloriously contented future* but I frowned instead. Anyway I didn't really care what Ray thought. I was going to pretend I'd stopped writing it. Got bored. Too *doomy*. Tip tip, tappety tap.

16: Of course I did

Tracey didn't come home until ten o'clock the next morning. I was in the lounge huddled over a plate of mashed potato; I don't know how long it'd been in the fridge but I fried it up anyway. I can't have cooked it long enough because it was still cold in the middle.

I'd lain in bed for an hour or so, dehydrated and displaced, and short of killing myself, the only other option was to get out of bed. The sheets had blood on them, and there was some on the pillow. It made me cringe to look at it. Tracey's gown was on the floor at the end of the bed, but I didn't want to look at the sleeve to see how badly stained it was – I threw it into the bottom of the wardrobe instead, trying to pretend that this was a casual gesture, the casual gesture of a woman getting up. (If you'd been watching me you would have believed that: you might have thought I was a rather tired-looking woman in her thirties – what were those cuts on her arm? – getting up and padding around a messy bedroom, picking something up off the floor and tossing it into the wardrobe.)

I heard Tracey's key in the lock and her footsteps coming down the hall, and stared ferociously at my plate. She walked around the house for a while, going to the toilet and into the bedroom, and then I heard her coming towards the lounge.

I made my eyes blur into the mashed potato.

"Hello," she said.

She still had her pink dress on which gave her the air of an exotic lap dancer fallen down a rabbit's hole. Her eyeliner was becomingly smudged, and her blonde hair fabulously tousled. She looked like a recently fucked movie star.

"I stayed the night," she said.

"Did you?"

"*I knew you'd be like that.* You can believe what you want. Where's Polly?"

"You slept on the couch, did you?"

"No. I slept on a mattress in the lounge."

"Bullshit."

"*I did.*"

"I don't believe you."

"I couldn't get home because you took the car and I had no money. You were so rude. It was so *embarrassing.* Where's James?"

"So you decided you'd stay the night, did you?"

"I just told you."

"And you slept on a mattress? In the lounge?"

"Yes. *I told you.* I don't have to convince you."

"Well, considering you didn't even know the guy before you met me –"

"Oh, don't be so stupid!"

"Did he have enough blankets, did he?"

"Yes thank you. Where's Polly?"

"How the fuck would I know? Did you talk about me?"

"What do you expect? You don't behave like that and then –"

"What did you say? What did Martin say?"

"*I don't know.* Did you feed the cat?"

"Yes."

"What did she have?"

"Sardines."

"I smelt those in the bedroom," she said brightly.

"You slept with him, didn't you?"

"*No.* I don't want to talk about it –"

"How convenient."

"I'm getting changed."

She rushed off to the bedroom, and I sat there, still with my half-eaten plate of cold mashed potatoes on my lap. Maybe she didn't sleep with him. She was supposed to be gay wasn't she? My hands were shaking. I wasn't going to let her see my arm. If I could just get through the day maybe it'd be OK tomorrow. Maybe it was just a hangover. But what if she fucked him? I couldn't stand it. I went into the bedroom where she was putting some trousers on.

"Tracey. Please. I need to know if you slept with him."

She sat on the edge of the bed with a sigh, and looked me directly in the eye.

"No."

"Really?"

"*No*," she said, now irritated.

"Thank you."

"That's all right." She buttoned up her trousers and looked around for a top to put on.

"I went out with James so I'd be out when you got back," I said.

Her eyes narrowed.

"I'm sorry about last night," I said, "I feel terrible today."

"You look it. Do you want to go out and have breakfast?"

"No... I don't know. Why? Do you?"

She pulled a spangly little number over her head. "Yeah. Maybe."

"How did you get home anyway?"

"I got a taxi. Martin put it on the business or something."

Fuck she was stupid.

"Then why didn't you get one last night?" I demanded.

"*Ohh*. Give it a rest. Guess what?"

"What?"

"I've got a job! At Producers/Directors! Nigel offered it to me."

I couldn't look at her.

"I start tomorrow," she said, going over to one of her piles of clothes. "Trainee Assistant Director. Not Martin," she added quickly, "another director. Martin's doing a documentary."

"Great."

There wasn't much to say after that. Tracey tried to suppress her good mood, but she didn't try too hard – after all, she still had the upper hand: I was the one who had run off and slammed the door in her face. But, for all that, she was overcompensating like mad – or rather, she was *overacting*. I got dressed, not daring to look at myself in the mirror, while she raced around folding reams of clothing and cleaning out the dirt box. She chattered on, careful to avoid the subject of Martin and her new job and what I did last night – which didn't give her an awful lot to talk about. She soon exhausted the topic of what to wear on her first day at work.

"I'm hungry," she said. "*Starving.*"

After a good night's fucking I expect you would be.

So, I was now to be serving girl, production manager, pale accountant.

"Would you like to go out for something to eat?" I said coldly.

"Ye-es!" (*You get the boat Julian and I'll round up the others!*)

There followed a flurry of hair teasing, and deciding what shoes to wear, and wondering where the cat was. I questioned her all the way to the coffee shop. *I bet you did sleep with him.* (No.) *Come on, you can tell me, I won't mind.* (There's nothing *to* tell.) *Please tell me Tracey.* (I've *told* you. I slept in the lounge.)

I was convinced she was telling the truth by the time the bell tinkled over the door of the cafe.

"Hello!" Tracey called to the Frenchman behind the counter.

"'Ello!" he hailed back, both of them several continents away from my own state of mind. I ordered coffee, and Tracey went for grilled bacon, poached eggs, hash browns and croissants, with a pot of tea. As usual she didn't have any money.

"If you pay for it now, I'll pay you back when I get paid," she said.

My arm hurt.

"Is your hand still sore?" she asked when I winced as I tried to find a pen in my bag.

"Yes."

"It looks all right."

"Mm."

When I opened my cheque book I saw that I'd not only paid the cab by cheque but I'd filled out the cheque stub as well. Good grief.

We sat down. It was better being out than being at home, at least. I heaped sugar into my coffee while she poured her tea. A man having breakfast looked up from his newspaper and watched her, rubbing his tongue absent-mindedly against his front teeth as he did so. I waited to see if he was going to look at me as well, but he didn't.

Tracey tucked into her brunch while I got myself another coffee and stared at a Sunday paper. As usual, being with Tracey made me feel relentlessly alone. She rubbed her leg against mine.

"Hello you," she said, ripping off a hunk of croissant and buttering it lavishly. "Are you going back to work this week?"

"Probably."

"We can get ready together." She reached over and covered my hand with hers. "It's all right," she said. "Don't worry. Here. Have some of my croissant."

"A croissant's not going to solve my problems."

She looked at me understandingly. "No."

"*What?* You think I've got problems?"

"*No.*"

She ate the rest of her croissant without speaking, then said, "Where did you go last night anyway?"

"I went out with James."

"That's good." She took a mouthful of tea. "Ahh," she said. "That's better."

"So how was dinner?"

She looked at me warily. "OK."

"What did you talk about?"

"Nothing really."

"Did you talk about me?"

"Not really..." She paused, and I couldn't quite read the emotion – jealousy? Superiority? "Martin told us what you did one night when he was editing –"

Embarrassment whipped at me, and I tried to cover it by picking up my coffee.

"Editing?"

"Yeah. Some girl."

"*What?*"

(What girl? What was she talking about?)

"There was a girl working there. Laura? Lorna? You tried to kiss her –"

"I didn't –"

"Apparently, yeah. You had your arm around her and you wanted her to come home with you and Martin –"

"I did not!"

(Of course I did. No question about it.)

"And you tried to kiss her –"

"I didn't."

"Mmm," she said. "Martin said she got really angry –"

"Oh my God. You're kidding."

Everything I thought about myself was true. My face turned crimson and then an underground shade of grey, and then the only colour, the only life about me, as I sat there in my bubble watching Tracey finish her tea, watching the man with the newspaper, watching the Frenchman bustling about in his apron – the only colour about me was the blood red, the stupid cuts hardening across my arm.

17: Oddly empty

After we got home Tracey was actively indifferent to any angst on my behalf, and spent the rest of the day alternating between looking for the cat, talking on the phone, and getting her clothes ready for work, while I mooched around the house beating myself up at every available opportunity.

She wanted to have the entire week planned out, down to the last sock. Or stocking, or tights, or whatever she was teaming up with what. Monday she was going to wear a full-length wool skirt with black shoes, a fluffy jacket and gold necklace. Hair down. Or what about... *up?* Betwixt trotting outside to look for Polly and making cups of tea she painted her nails and toenails bright red, and when they were dry she changed her mind and took it all off again. James didn't surface until it was dark, and then came into the lounge briefly to make a phone call before going out again. We didn't speak to one other. I nodded at him, and he gazed at me and rubbed his suppurating nose, and then reached inside it, into one of the collapsing cavities, to extract a shovelful of the previous night's excesses, before dumping it on the floor and reaching for the phone.

Tracey began planning Cat Missing notices for the neighbourhood lampposts. She made phone call after phone call to her friends who sympathised about the cat and congratulated her on her good fortune and asked after me.

I was in a daze for most of the day: Prozaced and painkillered. Palliated. All the Ps.

I went to bed at eight o'clock, and Tracey crept in and out with various garments, and walked around carrying the phone, doing odd jobs while she talked to people. I fell asleep to a series of *I know's!* and *Me too's!* and *Thanks!*

She was up at the crack of dawn showering and making breakfast.

"How are you feeling today?" she said as I came into the kitchen. She'd done the dishes and made some toast. "I can't believe I'm starting work today."

"No."

"Have you got a problem with that?"

"No. It was just very sudden, that's all."

"So? They were looking for someone."

She cut a piece of toast in half and offered it to me.

"No thanks."

"Please yourself. Are you going to work today?"

"Yes."

I went back to the bedroom. All I wanted was for her to acknowledge that if she hadn't known me she wouldn't have had a bloody job. A small thank you might do. I didn't think that was too much to ask for, considering I was paying her rent and buying her food and she was supposed to *love me*, wasn't she? What was all that about?

I couldn't believe she was working at Martin Myers's work. Good fucking luck to her, I muttered to myself as I got dressed. I hoped she had a wonderful fucking time and got paid millions and met exciting wonderful people, while I made life easier for Liz Fuckface PUBLIC RELATIONS.

"What are you saying?" she said, coming in behind me.

"Nothing."

She sprayed my perfume liberally over herself and then held the bottle up and said, "Do you mind if I use this?"

"No."

"How do I look?"

"Lovely."

After she left I drove to work and parked next to the radio van. Having to get out of the car seemed insurmountable. I was wearing a long-sleeved polo neck (a small victory) – mainly to cover the cuts on my arm – and I'd gone overboard on the foundation to conceal the ink rings under my eyes. Danny Wayne drove up and parked next to me.

"Good morning!" he said. He looked so pleased with himself that I wanted to *be* him. "The big meeting this morning." He got his brief-case out of the back of the car and looked around the car park. "It's all very hush hush," he said, "but I'm doing breakfast as of next week."

"That's good."

"Keep it to yourself."

We walked to the car park lift.

"Thanks for those trips you gave me," I said.

He made a gesture of mock innocence and said, "What trips were they?"

"What was in them?"

He laughed and the lift doors opened and he checked to make sure no one was inside, which I took to be a signal that he was going to tell me. We got in and he adjusted his tie and looked straight ahead. I was still looking at him, waiting for an answer, when the lift doors opened at reception.

"I don't know doll," he said as he got out. "*Hey*, Max!"

Maxine complimented him on his suit, and tried to get a look at me as I walked quickly to the stairs. I knew Liz wasn't in because her car hadn't been downstairs. As I unlocked our door, Mace came up the stairs holding his motorcycle helmet and an apple. We said hi and I went into the office and looked around. Nine-thirty. Tracey would be arriving now. First day. New girl. Martin Myers. Fucking bitch.

The phone rang.

"It's Maxine. How *are* you? Are you all right?"

"Yeah."

"Come down and see me. Oops. Better not."

Liz must have come in. Maxine hung up, and I sat at my desk and waited for Liz. My desk was a mess. Everything had been moved. There were some phone numbers on my blotter. Not Liz's handwriting. I heard Liz coming up the stairs, and looked into my rubbish bin.

"I wondered if you'd be here," she said. I watched her back as she walked purposefully to her desk. Navy suit. Must be going out.

She coughed and straightened some papers and picked up the phone and then put it down again.

"You and I need to have a talk," she said.

Boom diddy boom diddy boom.

"I'm busy this morning, but this afternoon. You could please ring Greg Agnew and confirm our meeting. And I'd like some coffee please."

Big serious one. Liz normally made her own coffee.

"Get some money out of petty cash."

She wanted me to go down to the coffee shop at the end of the road and bring one back for her. Deep shit.

I got some money and closed the office door on my way out, and then sneaked across the corridor to see Mace. He was sitting at his computer making small whistling noises through his teeth.

"Woo hoo!" he said, looking at me like I knew what the fuck he was doing. I had to sit beside his fermenting armpits looking interested for the next ten minutes, watching him drag boxes around the screen before enough time had gone by to ask him for a smoke. *Yeah yeah*, he said but didn't stop. I started panicking about getting Liz's coffee and was about to leave when he got his tin out. We stood by the open window and secretly smoked our way through a joint and then he diddled on for a few more minutes before I finally managed to escape. Once outside I wasn't sure I wanted to escape. I should have been back already by now. And I probably stunk of dope.

Fuck I was stoned. I had to go into the coffee shop. Please don't let there be anybody in there I know. I soldiered my way down the road, staving off panic.

Danny Wayne was in there with the new Programme Director, deep in conversation. I stood in the queue, praying they wouldn't look up, my mouth getting drier and drier. It was my turn at the counter. I tried to say cappuccino but couldn't get the word out and turned and walked out instead. I remembered what the ambulance woman had said – that if I felt like I was going to hyperventilate again I should just get up and start running. It stabilised your oxygen intake or something. I broke into a sweaty trot back to work and kept running past the front door, round the back to the car park.

Liz would be wanting her coffee. Fuck it. This was ridiculous. I walked back out onto the street again and went back to the coffee shop.

This small act of personal bravery stabilised me slightly, to the point where I became aware of myself again.

I ordered the cappuccino, paid for it and half-ran back to the office. I must have been squeezing the polystyrene cup too tightly because cinnamon froth was coming out of the hole in the lid. I stopped and tried to wipe it off with my hand.

Forty minutes after first leaving, I rushed through reception, up the stairs and into the office. I was about to apologise when Liz said, "Get out."

"Pardon?"

"You heard me, just get out. Take your things."

"What do you mean?"

"Look *get out* Ruth. Go home. We'll talk about it tomorrow."

She got up and walked out of the office herself.

I was shocked, but not altogether surprised by this latest turn of events. I continued to stand there, my thoughts chased into that small bruised corner that exists for occasions such as these. I went to see Mace.

"Do you want this?" I said, holding out the coffee. "I think Liz is mad with me."

"Ah," he said, looking at me curiously like I was already a thing of the past. "She's been on the warpath."

He took the coffee and went back to the screen, closing off any *what am I going to do now* conversations. I didn't know what the legal position was: she probably had to warn me first, or put it in writing or something. My phone rang. Going to get it seemed like a positive response.

"It's Maxine. What *happened?*"

By the tone of her voice it was obvious she'd known all along. The whole fucking world was probably in on it. Tracey probably knew as well.

"I've got to go. Talk to you later," I said and put down the phone. Then picked it up and slammed it down again. Then got up and locked the door and started crying. *Again*. What next? Beelzebub swaggering in with a job offer? Or something a little more proverbial? A plague of locusts perhaps? I glanced at the window and thought about putting a towel under the door to keep them out.

"Thank God you're there. It's Tracey. Maxine's just rung me."

"How's work going?"

"It's great! Well, it's *all right*. Look I'm going to come home early. Maxine and I are going to take you out to dinner – I'll pay. Hold on Ruth. Just a minute... What's that Nigel?... Yep. Yep. I've got to go, Ruth. I'll be home about six." She paused, waiting for an answer. "Otay?"

You'd think she was personally responsible. But that was the thing with Tracey. Everything had to revolve around her. And if it didn't she simply ripped it out of its orbit and made sure it did.

When the phone rang, I'd been sitting on the couch knitting like a maniac. I'd driven home in the late morning traffic: it felt like one of those days when you'd been to the dentist and were on your way back to school. Oddly empty. I put the knitting back in its bag. Let Tracey finish the fucking thing.

I looked at my arm. Maybe being at home wouldn't be such a bad idea. It wouldn't hurt to have some time off anyway. Think about what direction my life was taking. Something must have been occurring in the cosmos for so much chaos to be visited upon one person. Surely it must signify something. And all that stupid fucking business with the man in the tracksuit. Maybe I was schizophrenic and he was just some sick part of my psyche conjured up by chemicals? *Ruth's gone now. Willy's here now. Say hello to Willy.*

I stood looking out the window. It was overcast outside. I thought about being on a desert island with Martin Myers, him in a pair of shorts, we both trying to light a fire, no hope of rescue for at least six months. An image of Tracey in a helicopter waving and shouting *hello!* put paid to that and I went into the bedroom. I lay on the bed and contemplated masturbating, but it wasn't worth the effort: I could lay there wanking all day and just end up with a sore finger. No more Prozac. No more pot. No more alcohol. No more nothing.

Sure. I'd been down that road before. And what was I going to do instead? Eat? Take up swimming? Poison another cat? (*Kitten* Ruth, *kitten*.)

Maybe it wasn't dead. I had no idea what ten Prozac did to a cat – it might be having a great time for all I knew.

Unlikely.

I turned the radio on. Life was going on without me. I wondered if they knew at the radio station that I'd gone. Danny Wayne might say something on air. I moved Tracey's things out of the hall and stacked them up haphazardly outside the spare bedroom.

I rang Producers/Directors but Martin was out. I left a message for him to call me then rang the direct studio line at the station.

"Hi Danny. It's Ruth –"

He put me on the speaker phone. "Yeah?" he yelled from the back of the studio. I could hear him going through the cart racks, getting his ads together for the next break.

"Did you hear about what happened?"

"Wait on – *Easy Listening HarmonyFM with Danny Wayne here with you right through till four. Good afternoon. News and weather on the hour* – Sorry. Hiya doll. Yeah, I start on Monday. Hey thanks for your call. Gotta go. Got the news coming up."

I sat on the couch looking through my address book. There were some ex-girlfriends in there. One old boyfriend. My parents. I wasn't going to ring them – they'd never even been to the flat. My father had rung once but my mother was keeping her distance since I'd drunkenly told her one night that I liked sleeping with women.

Listen! Don't tell me about it Ruth. What you do in your own time is your own business, but I don't want it in this house.

I snooped around in a box of Tracey's things and read a few letters written to her from Alicia. Lengthy descriptions of holiday activities, the need to get away, the missing you.

I was dressed and ready to go to dinner at six o'clock. Tracey burst in the front door at half past with Maxine and Mace (Mace?) behind her and sat down and immediately started knitting before she'd even taken her coat off. Maxine made everyone a cup of tea, and Mace sat on the couch like Humpty Dumpty, goggling at Tracey.

"I don't believe it," Tracey said, gripping the needles. "What are you going to do?"

"I don't know. Leave. You look like you should be sitting in front of a guillotine. Are you coming out with us Mace?"

"Yeah," Tracey answered for him. "That's OK isn't it? God, I'm exhausted." She wrenched some more wool out of the bag.

"How was your day? Did you see Martin?" I said.

"Yep. Yep. He was good."

"I left a message for him," I said.

"*Did* you?" she said. "Hey, you'd really like Nigel. He's amazing. He's *so* talented. And he's such a laugh. He used to be a director in the eighties…"

(And on it went…)

Dinner was uneventful. I didn't have to go to hospital. I remembered it all.

We went to a Thai restaurant and Tracey sat me down between her and Maxine. Mace sat on the other side of the table and gazed at us fondly. I told them I wasn't going back to work and Tracey touched my hand protectively and ordered for me. Tracey and Maxine tried to come up with band names and I laughed along, thinking what bastards they were. It was Tracey's birthday coming up and they talked about having a party, and then cancelled that idea in favour of going out to dinner.

Mace fidgeted and tried to look intellectual. He got a notebook out of his bag and wrote something in it and Tracey looked at him approvingly. She treated him like the family pet, scratching him behind the ears every now and then. I couldn't work out what he was doing there.

I ended up paying for dinner because Tracey's first pay wasn't for a few weeks. We couldn't get rid of Mace. He wanted to come back to the flat and keep drinking. Tracey and Maxine both had work in the morning, which was a good excuse to drop him at a taxi stand. I knew he knew Tracey was gay. Maybe he just thought he'd try his luck anyway.

I got changed in the bathroom when we got home so Tracey wouldn't see my arm. She set the alarm and went out the back and called for Polly for a while. She wanted to have sex when we got into bed. The old arm creeping thing. I said I couldn't. Overtired. Prozac.

"Don't worry," she said. "You'll get another job. Turn over?"

"I just want to go to sleep."

She lay there for a while, cross, but soon curled up and fell asleep, purring with the prospect of day two as Gorgeous Trainee Assistant Director, Tracey May.

Too bad about me, eh?

18: Hermes and Aphrodite

It was winter then and it's winter again now. Just starting. A few leaves blowing here and there. A general battening down of the hatches. When I began writing this all those months ago I knew how the story ended up (in regard to Tracey) but I didn't know how *I* would end up.

I got a postcard today, from Dee in Bangkok – a picture of a huge reclining Buddha. On the back she's written *I'm afraid I didn't take to it at all. I'm probably too old, or too male, or both.* I couldn't figure out what the fuck she was talking about and then I remembered where I'd seen it before. Another one of her rejection letters. I spent the morning wondering why she had it in for me. What did I represent to her? Her own failure? I burned the bloody thing.

Unfortunately Ray arrived while I was doing it. I told him what she'd written and he made some crack about my persecution complex coming along nicely then. He thinks I should go and see another psychiatrist. Personally I don't think there's much a psychiatrist could do except call the police. He thinks I'm *troubled*. That's a joke. Christ. His life's not exactly normal. And there's the rub – I don't need a psychiatrist to tell me that – it's been a quest, all my life mostly, for normality. And never knowing what the benchmark is. What I should be measuring it against. When you're in your own box you imagine all sorts of loving encounters going on next door. It's pathetic. A lifetime spent wondering what the people next door are up to.

I wonder what Nastassja Kinski's up to right now? What she looks like when she wakes up in the morning?

That's pathetic as well. If Nastassja Kinski was going to be in love with anybody it'd be a *man*. Nastassja Kinski is a male fantasy. Man. Male. Mister.

Maybe men fell for her because they liked the duality of her. The beautiful boy aspect. The handsome girl. *She was a fine and handsome girl*. Hardy couldn't have said it better: Tess couldn't have been played by anyone *but* her. And that naked prowl through *Cat People*. My God. Essentially female but complicated with a male directness. The son of Hermes and Aphrodite. The Ultimate Bisexual.

Maybe I should start a fanzine.

Give me something to do on the plane.

I knew James was depraved, but I didn't know the true extent of it until I saw it first-hand. Because he did shift work at the restaurant he was often at home during the day, and his first mission upon waking was to source the day's orgasm. He was very organised, usually working a day or two ahead of himself. There was always a boy on midterm break, or a drug deal paid for begrudgingly in his bedroom, or someone he'd picked up on a lunch shift and booked in for the following week. If all else failed he kept the street kids who hung around the back of the sports centre in reserve. He quickly got over his annoyance at finding out that I was going to be at home during the day, cottoning on to the fact that I could be useful in providing an impression of ordinariness if he spent a few minutes introducing me and offering coffee before herding his catch down the hall.

I went to bookshops and read about hyperventilation and depression. I rang Maxine who said Liz was waiting for me to call her and that she wanted my keys back. She was going to get Maxine to type me a letter *outlining my position.* I rang Martin two or three times and left messages. Tracey said he was busy on his documentary and no one had seen him. She phoned me several times a day to see how I was, and tried to play down how much she was enjoying her new job. She saw the cuts on my arm one night and pulled me over to the light to have a look at them with the new found confidence of a Trainee Assistant Director. She didn't ask how they'd got there but gave me a searching look and then went and made salad and pork chops for dinner. She borrowed my car one night to go round to Maxine's for their first band practice but didn't ask me if I wanted to go. Her friends started coming around in shifts: a girl from college fishing around for a job at Producers/Directors, a solo mum whose four-year-old presented Tracey with chocolates for her birthday, one of the gawky male directors from work. I smiled and made jokes and showed them round the flat. Excellent reports started coming in about me.

It was my turn to make the tea apparently. When I came back with it Tracey was lying in bed looking at her postcards on the dressing table mirror.

"Which woman would I fancy if I could have any one of them?" she asked.

"I don't know. The dark-haired one," I said.

"No."

"I don't know."

"Guess."

"The one on the beach – ?"

"No."

I handed her her tea. "I like the one on the beach."

"I don't," she said, and then looked at me, trying to gauge my level of animosity.

"I meant to ask you –" I stopped momentarily. The brown velvet gown had been unearthed in one of Tracey's clothes-mining expeditions. I chucked a pair of trousers nonchalantly on top of it. "– What was Mace doing there the other week when we went to dinner?"

"Mace? Nothing. He just came along."

"Why?"

"He was going to design some posters for me – for Polly," she said. "Anyway, what are you going to do today?"

There was something odd about the way she changed the subject. She was covering up for something.

"Guess what?" she said.

Tracey liked these guessing games. They were always about her.

"What?"

"I'm going to have lunch with Nigel today."

"How surprising."

"*What?*" She glared at me.

I decided to say it. It'd been on my mind.

"Tracey, are you just stupid or do you just pretend to be?"

"Are you just horrible or do you just pretend to be?" she said back.

"Both."

I looked around the room, then at her.

"Sorry," I said.

Better not rile her too much.

She got out of bed and started to sort through the day's costume.

"Do you want some more tea?" I asked her.

"Yes please."

"Where are you going for lunch then?"

She was hauling up her gold-trimmed knickers, and stopped and looked at me excitedly.

"Whites," she said, reaching for a lace vest.

Whites was a dimly lit advertising hang-out which was usually reserved for dinner without your wife.

"That'll be nice. Will you be home tonight?"

"Yep. I'll cook," she said, pulling on her stretch lilac trousers.

"You won't be that hungry, will you?" I said, taking her cup. "All that sperm."

She gave me a withering look and sat on the bed to put her shoes on.

After she'd gone I went to see if James was home. His door was closed but he was in there. I could smell him. I knocked and opened the door. He was in bed, snoring. "Are you awake? James?" I shook his shoulder.

He rolled over and pulled the blankets around his neck. His pillow-case was soft with dirt. There was a tube of lubricating jelly and some chocolates on the chair by his bed. I had one and flicked the wrapper at his head on the way out.

Liz called wanting to know when I was going to come in with my keys. I told her I was leaving and she said *that's probably for the best* and asked me to bring my keys in. I said *yeah maybe* and hung up. Maxine called soon after.

"It's Max. What did you say to Liz? She's furious."

"She wants me to bring my keys in. How are you? Are you missing me?"

"You have to stop that now. You've got Tracey."

"I'd rather have you."

She laughed fetchingly. "No you wouldn't."

"Wouldn't I?"

"No. I've got to go. There's some competition on."

"Thanks for coming out to dinner."

"Dinner? Don't be silly. I wanted to."

"What was Mace doing there?" I chortled.

"I *know*. Poor Tracey. You should see the faxes he sends her – God, these phones."

"You better go," I said. "Phone me later."

And just what faxes were they?

Hmmm?

Just as I was going out the door a courier arrived with a letter from Liz. It was a one-page diatribe which listed persistent absenteeism, unacceptable rudeness to clients and drug taking on the premises.

And this insistence on a man in a tracksuit dogging you really is too much Ruth.

Maxine looked surprised to see me. It was weird being there. No longer my territory.

"I'm leaving too," Maxine said when no one was in reception.

I was pleased. It cut off any last link with the place, and any regret

I might have about leaving myself.

"Where are you going?" (And somehow I knew before I'd even asked her.)

"Producers/Directors. Reception."

"Oh really? Tracey didn't mention it."

Like a lot of things.

"They want me to come in tomorrow for an interview. I'm taking the day off sick. Did you get your letter? I didn't want to type it. Liz made me."

"Is Liz here?" (I was going to ask if Mace was in as well, but thought better of it.)

"No. She's out for the afternoon."

"Good. I'll go up."

Maxine looked worried.

"What's the matter?"

"She said if you came in, not to let you –"

"Don't worry about it –"

"But –"

She looked genuinely scared. Of *me*.

"What? You want me to give you the keys?"

"No," she said plaintively.

"Look, just forget you saw me OK? Pretend I sneaked in. I'm only going to clean out my desk. What do you think I'm going to do? Smear faeces on the walls?"

"No," she said defensively, but I could see in her eyes that she thought I was capable of it. One of the sales reps rushed past and nodded at me.

"Someone's seen you now," Maxine said unhappily.

"Maxine, I'll be upstairs OK? Smearing shit on Liz's computer."

The door to Mace's office was open. They had a fax machine and I wanted to look around and see if I could find the mysterious faxes he'd been sending to Tracey. Andrew was in there working at the computer. Mace's leather satchel was on the floor.

"Hi Andrew – is Mace here?"

"He had to go home for something. He won't be long. How are things with you? I hear you're leaving?"

"Yeah."

"Do you want a cup of coffee?" I asked.

"Yeah, love one. I'll make it." He jumped up and picked up his mug.

"I was thinking about a real one –"

"Oh? Ah –"

"I'll go and get them," I said quickly, looking crestfallen. Redundant PA with no friends.

"No, no," he said emphatically. "No. I'll get them. What do you want?"

I calculated I had fifteen minutes tops. And Mace could come back at any minute. Nothing by the fax machine. Nothing on the tables. The filing cabinet was locked. I got Mace's satchel and crouched down behind the computer desk with it. Bills. An ideas folder. A brown manila folder, unmarked. I opened it. Producers/Directors letterhead. Tracey's signature. Bingo.

Five minutes had passed since Andrew left. I didn't know whether to read them or steal the folder. I put Mace's satchel back where I'd found it and took the folder over to our office and went in. There was a cardboard box sitting on my desk with all my stuff in it. I locked the door behind me and started to read the faxes. They were all filed in the order they were sent and received. The first one was sent on the day we went out for dinner. Tracey had faxed Mace asking her if he could put together a poster for the cat. Then there was a passage about an idea she had for a short film, suggesting to Mace that they could work on it together, and a *see you tonight* with a lipstick kiss, *love T.*

Love T?

Next fax: from Mace to Tracey. *So good to hear your voice girl. I'll send this at exactly 11am so you're standing by the fax machine. It was so hard (!) last night. Watching you at dinner and knowing you'll never be mine –*

What the fuck?

And then there was a *poem* about the blonde goddess stampeding through his dreams.

I was stunned. I couldn't believe what I was reading. What the fuck was Tracey up to? Obviously Mace had a crush on her but she must have encouraged it. And when did she get the time?

The faxes continued in this vein with Tracey playing up to him and Mace getting more and more verbose. Humorous quotes, poetry, passages from books, cartoons.

Then.

Then the one I couldn't take in.

Then the one that said: *Mace I really like you but it can't go any further than that right now. At the moment I'm thoroughly enjoying myself having an affair with a director at work. He is somewhat the maverick, a star. I don't know how it will end up, but right now it's what I need. You have to promise you won't tell Ruth. You promise?*

I read it again and again and again,

(there was no pain)

dumbfounded by my own naivety, dazed by the impact, sitting in the middle of the intersection with glass on my lap wondering why the steering wheel was sticking out of my knee.

(the pain comes later)

Trembling, I put all the faxes back into the folder (except the last one which I kept) and then returned it to Mace's satchel. Andrew came in thirty seconds later carrying coffee and pastries. I thanked him and had my coffee and made stilted conversation before thanking him again and going back to my desk. The immediate effect of Tracey's infidelity seemed to be one of obsequiousness. I got my cardboard box, and looked around for anything else that might be mine. Liz had my paperweight on her desk. I left it there. Let her have the whole fucking lot.

Maxine was on the phone when I got down to reception. My eyes were stinging, and I wasn't sure that looking at her was such a good idea, but I managed to mouth *thank you* and point to the box. She looked guilty and pointed at the telephone *I'll call you.* Then, *keys.*

I put my keys on her desk. I could hear Danny Wayne in the kitchen. On a high. The new breakfast jock. I went in to see him, aware of the great spill of emotion that was building up behind my ribcage. Danny was testing out a joke on one of the sales reps who laughed uproariously and then left, jacket flapping.

"Hiya doll," Danny said, laughing too, about to follow him out to look for the rest of the audience.

"You don't have any of those trips left, do you Danny?"

He scanned the corridor to see if anyone had heard. "Come down to the car park. Five minutes," he said and walked off, whistling.

While I waited for him all I could think about was Tracey and Martin Myers writhing around in bed. I pulled the fax out and looked at it again. I felt faint. Bloodless. *Don't worry love, the ambulance will be here soon.*

Mace drove in on his motorbike. He didn't see me and I had enough time to crush the fax up into my pocket. I didn't know what to do with my eyes. If he looked at me he would surely know that I'd been in his bag. That I had the fax.

He didn't seem to notice anything. He kept his helmet on as he came towards the lift. He was wearing leather trousers that were too tight for his fat legs. I registered that my obsequiousness was giving way to resentment – still passive, but building.

The lift doors opened and Danny Wayne got out. Mace had no option but to get in.

Danny was late for an appointment: we went straight to his car and he took a small plastic bag out from behind the sun visor. He said the trips had been given to him by a friend who was an airline steward, and this guy had had them in his freezer for years. He only had six left. I bought them all and as he was about to drive off he wound his window down and offered me some chewing gum. This ridiculous act of kindness was almost enough to send me over the edge.

As soon as he'd gone I read the fax again. I read it again in the car. Seeing it in black and white still didn't make it real somehow. I went over all the opportunities Tracey had had to have an affair – the night she stayed over obviously, but she hadn't spent any other nights away.

At work. She must have been lying about him not being around. They probably held hands over coffee each morning. Kissed behind tape racks. Fucked in toilets. You bitch.

(Funny how I never thought *you bastard*.)

I got home to an empty house – although someone had been there because I could smell cigarette smoke and the kettle was still warm. I scrabbled around looking through the ashtrays in case they were Martin Myers's cigarettes. They weren't, but anything was possible now. I unscrewed the fax and put it on the table and looked at it.

Thoroughly enjoying myself.

I bet she fucking was.

Oh, to have everything. To have everything available to you because of your looks. (I didn't want to admit, *couldn't*, that it might have been her personality as well that attracted people. How could I think that, when all I could think of her was that she was a lying two-faced selfish egotistical little fuck?)

Where does anger like this go? Where does it go? If you're normal I suppose you get it out of your system by talking, and screaming (all that *talking*), and accusing and breaking down: you sit outside McDonald's in the car savaging each other while the children cling to you, yelling, *stop Mummy!*, but you can't stop, up it comes again like the sick it is; and months later, sometimes years later, if there was still love there, if *you* were still there, you forgave, and you learnt from it. That's what they say, don't they? You've got a right to be angry, *but now you've got to let it go and learn from it. Move on.*

I didn't want to learn from it. What was I going to learn? That people betrayed you? That you let them in, and while you were making up a bed for them they were in the other room quietly helping themselves, taking what they wanted. Acting all goofy around your husband. They *wanted* those sweets, that dress. Your husband. They wanted your entire fucking life.

And I already knew (I knew because it didn't surprise me when it surfaced in my thoughts) that given the reverse set of circumstances I would have done exactly the same thing.

I was as rotten as she was.

But I squashed this thought; I pummelled it half to death then hid it in the basement and covered my ears when it whimpered.

I paced around the house cleaning up, emptying my cardboard box. My dictionary. Calculator. Stuff from my drawer. It looked like somebody else's.

I wavered like a faulty electric wire between action and inaction. I found some cigarettes and smoked one. It was disgusting: it made me so dizzy I had to lie down on the couch.

I was so angry with her I wanted to kill her.

Where does anger like this go?

It goes to stay with its parents, that's where.

19: A breath of air

I didn't take a coat. I didn't take a change of clothes. I left a note for Tracey saying *Gone out. love R.* If the irony was lost on her maybe she'd notice that I'd pressed so hard on the paper that the pen had gone through the word *love*.

She wouldn't notice a fucking thing. She'd just be pleased that she could ferret through my clothes in peace.

I hadn't been to my parents' new house but I knew my mother would be there. She was. She opened the door slowly, deeply discontented with what she might find behind it, even before she'd seen it. Her hair had gone completely grey in the six months since I'd last seen her. She was skinnier than ever, wearing jeans. Where do they make jeans that thin? She had a white sweatshirt on with a picture of a koala bear on it. She darted around sucking on boiled sweets and making the tea.

"So you've left work then?"

Everything my mother said sounded like an attack on me. It was the way she said it.

"Thinking about it," I said. "I haven't made up my mind. It's my holidays at the moment. I thought I might come and spend a few days with you?"

"You could have called first."

"Yeah sorry. I don't have to stay –"

"You're here now." She poured the tea and sat down.

"What have you been up to?" I asked.

Fuck all as usual. She did embroidery sometimes. Smoking was a big one. The house smelt like a pool hall. My mother had never worked. You didn't in her day. You had kids. She only ever had me, but she made a meal of it, like she did with everything.

"Not much. Your father's back's been playing up again."

"Have you got a spare room here?"

"You won't know will you, seeing as how you haven't been here," she said.

The house had all our old furniture in it, except they had a new lounge suite, and they'd put up framed photos of dogs they'd had over the years. There was a photo of me as well, above the telephone. It was an old school one.

"What did you put this up here for?"

"To remember what you look like," came the reply.

The spare room had the old double bed in it with the huge sag in the middle. On top of it were boxes of junk.

"There are some clean sheets in the hall cupboard," my mother said from the kitchen table. "I suppose you're still a vegetarian?"

What was I doing there? It was macabre. I decided I was only going to stay one night. I took the boxes off the bed and put them in the corner and made the bed. There was one blanket on it. I didn't ask for any more and my mother didn't offer. She was making roast chicken in honour of my appearance. I found an eiderdown in the hall cupboard, and tried to ignore the damp pillow as I put the pillowcase on it. It was a cheerless room and it suited me.

It was easy to deceive my mother: I'd been doing it all my life. I can't remember what we talked about, shit mostly, all the storage space she had now, when they last went to the races, the new coffee cups. I nearly went to the phone and rang Tracey but I stopped myself.

I wanted to ring Martin Myers, but I didn't want to alienate him. I clung to the notion that Tracey was a dalliance, that he would realise that *I* was the one, I was what he really needed.

Good god. I was thinking like a thirteen-year-old again.

Thirteen? Why did I always think *thirteen?*

My father came in at exactly five-thirty. He looked the same, like an undertaker with a pot-belly. He nearly hugged me, but didn't know how.

"Roast chicken," he said, sniffing the air. As if he hadn't had it every week for the last thirty-five years. He got a bottle of red wine from the wine rack I'd bought them one Christmas, and opened it.

"White with chicken," my mother said, watching him struggling with the bottle opener.

"I don't think it matters," he said.

We sat in the lounge with the roast chicken perched on our laps and watched the horse racing on cable TV. They were both so involved in it that they forgot about me. I ate quickly and drank as much wine as I could without them noticing, and then suggested we have another bottle. No one objected so I opened it in the kitchen and filled the biggest glass they had, a beer tankard. I poked my head around the corner of the lounge door. "I'm just going to get some fresh air," I said. "Is that OK?"

"All right love," my father said, smiling at me. My mother looked startled by this endearment and tried to smile too.

I went into the back garden and had a couple of puffs on a joint and then went back in.

"Is it all right if I have a bath?"

"Get a towel out of the hall cupboard," my mother said, watching the screen, holding her hand up to stop me from saying anything more as the horses crossed the line. "Yes! *Gotcha!*" she said. My father said *hee hee* and looked at me proudly and picked up the racing guide.

"Did you win?" I asked.

"Yes," my mother said tartly. "Didn't you like your dinner?"

"I ate it –" I protested.

"You didn't have very much."

"I had enough. It was delicious, thank you."

I went to the bathroom. My mother preferred showers to baths. She didn't like *lolling around* in the bath. This was a bath and shower in one and had a rubber mat in the bottom of it. The mat was dirty from where they'd been standing on it. I couldn't be bothered cleaning it out. Hair and other things floated around in the water as it filled up. I got undressed and lowered myself gingerly into it, noticing the mould on the wall tiles, and lay there with the shower curtain pulled across the length of the bath in case my mother came in for an inspection.

Did I really belong to these two? It was as if I'd gatecrashed someone else's house. The cuts on my arm had healed to leave six new pink scars. I got out and got dressed again, thinking I'd wear my clothes to bed to keep warm.

"I'm going to bed now."

"Goodnight," they both said, still watching TV, as if I'd never left home.

I sat up in the cold bed drinking my tankard of wine like medicine. I turned the light off and slept for a few hours. I dreamed – or maybe I thought about it – of a goldfish swimming in a plastic bag of water. Its bowl was being cleaned, and someone had put the goldfish in the plastic bag for safekeeping. But the knot holding the bag together hadn't been tied tightly enough and the water pressure was slowly splaying the bag open, slowly undoing the knot. Suddenly the whole thing opened up and collapsed, and the goldfish went flying over the edge of the bench and down into the gap between the stove and the bench.

It was obviously me, the goldfish. Even my symbolism was transparent. Everything about me was artless.

I spent the rest of the night awake and angry, thinking about Martin Myers and Tracey. I thought about them kissing and touching each other. I wondered what they said to each other. I imagined them cuddling up in his bed together. I cursed them and tried to cry, but couldn't for some reason.

I got up and had a cup of tea at about six o'clock and waited for my father to get up. He always made the tea before going to work. He looked pleased to see me there when he came out of the bedroom, sleepy and grey. He'd changed in the last ten years: he had some personality of his own now, even if it was weak. One last bid for personal liberty before the bell went.

We drank our tea at the kitchen table. I told him I was thinking about leaving my job. *What's that love?* he said, looking up from the morning paper. I poured a cup of tea for my mother and took it in.

It was still dark in their room. I opened the curtains and stood there with the tea. My mother saw it was me and sat up.

"Oh it's you," she said.

"I might get going today," I said. "I forgot, it's someone I know's birthday today."

She sniffed. "I knew it was too good to last," she said, taking her tea, her nightie giving off wafers of unpleasant sleep.

"Don't be so mean."

"I beg your pardon?" she said.

"You're always so mean to me."

I was scared, but I'd wanted to say it to her for years.

20: The clouds, the power lines, and the moon

She blinked once. Computer crash. I was about to say *I'm thirty-four years old*, when my father came in.

"I'm off now," he said. "What are your plans for the day, love?"

"Ah –" I picked up a bottle of perfume off the dressing table. It was sticky. Ancient.

"She's leaving," my mother said finally, putting down her tea.

"It's a friend's birthday party. I forgot."

"Oh." My father looked at my mother. "That's a shame," he said.

Now for the awkward bit. He never kissed my mother goodbye, or hello, or at any other time that I could remember, so I didn't expect that, but I could tell he was going to try out some form of bodily contact on me.

"Do you want some more tea?" I asked my mother, moving closer into the bed.

"No thank you," she said. "I'm getting up."

My father and I both turned our eyes away from her thin struggle out of bed, and then the moment for kissing was no more.

Poor old dad. He of the parched lips.

I felt sorry for them both. I felt sorry for myself. Fucking life. What's the point?

I got back home in the afternoon. Tracey was on the phone, a huge smile on her face. It jumped ship the instant she saw me. "Ruth's here, I've got to go," she said. She listened for a moment. "Thank you. That's nice. See you tonight."

"Martin Myers?" I said.

She looked like a frightened mouse.

"He's coming to dinner."

"Happy birthday," I said and went down the hall into the bedroom.

She didn't come near me. I stood in the middle of the room waiting for her but she went into the kitchen and stayed there. The bedroom had been cleaned up and there were flowers on the dressing table and about a hundred birthday cards. One from Maxine – a hand-painted one of a cat chasing a butterfly, and a teddy bear one from James. He didn't bother buying me a card on my birthday. The brown velvet gown was hanging up in the wardrobe, near the front. I heard Tracey coming towards the bedroom. She had a wooden spoon in her hand.

"I took the day off," she said, looking at the spoon. "I'm making rice pudding."

"Why?"

"For my birthday," she said hopefully. "I finished Martin's jersey for you."

"You can give it to him tonight then."

"You can."

"I'm sure he'd prefer it coming from you."

"Oh *shut up*. I'm fucking sick of you," she said, and stormed out, slamming the kitchen door when she got there.

I went out and got in the car and drove off. I didn't know where I was going. Anywhere. Away from her. If it had been possible I would have driven away from myself. I went and sat in a coffee shop for an hour looking out the window until the anger changed to self-pity. I went to a bookshop and surprised myself when a teardrop landed on the page beneath me. I bought the book. It was on creative visualisation. How to have good things come into your life. How to let go of all accumulated guilt, fears, resentment, disappointments and grudges of the past. How to forgive and release.

I went back to the car and dropped a trip, a whole one, swallowing it like a tired old spider, thinking about my life, about Tracey, about the man in the tracksuit, thinking: *Come on you bastard, come and get me.*

***

It was starting to come on when I got back. I went inside and went into my room and found some old wrapping paper, and hid it in my bag with the book. Tracey was in the kitchen. She'd been crying.

"Have we got any Sellotape?" I asked.

She wiped her nose and smiled weakly at the inference to presents. "I think so," she said. "In the drawer." She found the Sellotape and put her arms around me.

I stood there rigidly.

"Thanks for coming home," she said.

"It's your birthday isn't it? I've just had a trip, do you want one?"

She let go of me and looked at me tenderly.

"OK."

I went and got her a trip and watched her chew it up.

"We better eat this rice pudding now," she said, "otherwise we won't want it. I'll go and get changed. Are you all right now?"

"I feel a bit weird actually."

"It'll be fun. Everyone's coming. Can you dish up the pudding?"

I did as I was told. I got the plates out of the cupboard and dished up two creamy piles. It had raisins in it. I waited until it had cooled and then got the nail scissors and the other four trips and cut them up into minute pieces and mixed them into Tracey's pudding. I wrapped the book up. She was putting on her eyeliner in the bedroom mirror when I went in.

"I think mine's coming on already," she laughed. She looked like a fish. With a big open orange mouth. When she spoke her words came out in speech bubbles. I gave her her present and her pudding.

I am eight. Mary Smilovich is thirteen. We have been left alone for the day, and probably most of the night, while our parents go to the races. They say they'll be home at six but we all know they won't be. What freedom! The house is new and the Smiloviches have a big kitchen with an automatic washing machine in the corner. Mary has to do all the washing and hang it out. Her brother Kevin is bored. He's been playing upstairs and now he's going outside. He gets on his bike and says he's going to his friend's house.

I don't know Mary that well. She lives in another town and I only see her when our parents get together. Our parents are old friends from years ago. Her sister Rachel is a pain, hanging around me and Mary, and grizzling about not being allowed to go to her friend's if Kevin is allowed to go to his.

Mary tells her to go if she wants. And don't come back she yells after her, stuffing some more washing into the machine. I help her carry the basket out to the clothes line and we peg it up. I love taking the socks out and the towels and the underwear and looking at it all as I hang it up. I hang it up neatly, all joined together with pegs, over-lapping. Rows of red-and-blue-striped tea towels, we've got some of the red ones, and her father's work clothes and her mother's nightie. There is no more room on the line. Some of the earlier washing is dry. I offer to take it inside and start the ironing. The sun is hot, we're sweating. Mary's got brown arms with white silky hairs, and long brown legs. She's wearing Bermuda shorts. My own shorts have embroidery on them. I like these shorts and the red checked sleeveless top my mother made me. There are daisies on the lawn and a wheel-barrow. We get our towels and lie on the lawn with our faces in the sun. It's bright. You look at the sun and close your eyes and then open them and all you can see is the sun. I make a daisy chain for some-thing to do, carefully splitting the thin juicy stems with my fingernail, excited when I find a fat one. It breaks when I put it over Mary's head so I fix it for her.

We go inside and Mary makes banana sandwiches and takes a big bottle of Coke out of the fridge. Coke. I never have Coke. I have orange drink which my mother mixes in a plastic jug with water.

Her brother comes back with his friends. There are four of them. They ride their bikes up the drive, talking loudly and throwing their bikes in the new carport. They come in and grab the Coke and raid the bread bin. I am fascinated by this. Having a brother. Or even a sister. Mary seems to think nothing of it. She hates them, she says. She's bored. Do I smoke? The boys all howl with excitement.

Mary says we're going to put on a show, and tells the boys to go into the front room and close the curtains. No way they laugh and then do it, swigging on the Coke and wolfing down the bread.

What are we doing? I ask her in her bedroom.

Watch, she says. She takes her shorts off and then peels off her top. She is brown and naked and smiles at me. She puts on a dressing gown but doesn't do up the belt, she leaves the belt open so I can see underneath it, and pushes her hips at me.

Go on, she says.

What?

Take your clothes off.

What if someone comes?

They won't. Come on. She closes the blind and watches me until I take off my shorts and then my undies. The white ones with pink flowers. I stand there with nothing on. She laughs at me and finds me something to wear, her brother's dressing gown which is scratchy. I wear it exactly the same way she does. We go into the lounge and everyone looks at us. Mary closes the curtains and puts a record on and tells them all to sit on the couch. Her brother's eyes are popping out of his head. Mary says if anyone tells they'll be in big trouble. Everyone says they won't tell, and I stand beside Mary trying to copy her dancing. She pushes her hips forward and thrusts her brown stomach at her brother and his friends. I do the same. They watch and don't say anything. One of the boys looks scared but he doesn't stop watching. She takes off her dressing gown and dances around in front of them with no clothes on so I do the same. I have no clothes on. I push my body at them like Mary. I look at Mary but she's stopped dancing. She says she's bored. She puts on her dressing gown and turns the music off and says for me to follow her. We go back to her room and close the door.

I'm going swimming, she says and gets her bikini out of a drawer. Do you want to come?

I haven't got anything to wear.

Wear this. She passes me another bikini from the drawer. It's a halter-neck one with pink and purple patterns. We go downstairs again and walk past the boys with our noses in the air. I have to ride a boy's bike which hurts because my legs are too short for the pedals and I keep banging against the bar. Mary rides in front of me, faster than me, then wheels back and waits for me to catch up.

Where are the pools? I ask her.

We're going to the river, she says and rides on ahead, her brown legs pumping at the pedals. She has our towels on the back of her bike on the carrier. I'm hot. I don't want to ride anymore and then we're there. The grass is long and green and soft against my legs. It's quiet in the trees. I follow Mary towards the bridge pushing the bike through the grass. I can see the river. It's brown. It looks dirty. I don't want to swim in it. I want to go to the pools. I can hear birds overhead, jumping between branches, and the sun is dappled on my arm.

We get to the bridge and there's a tarpaulin in the undergrowth. There's a man there. I am about to say Run! when Mary says it's all right. The man has got white hair and a dog. It's a Doberman. I know it's a Doberman because my uncle has got one the same. It growls at us and the man clicks his fingers and it stops growling and lies on the tarpaulin in the shade, panting. The man looks like he's been playing indoor basketball. He's got a tracksuit on. He offers Mary a cigarette and she takes one and then he looks at me and holds out the packet. He laughs when I shake my head and then looks at Mary's towel.

Going swimming? he asks.

After this, she says, flicking ash into the bushes.

Let's go, I say and start to walk off. Mary says See ya and I keep walking towards the river like I know where I'm going. I flick my hair like she does and we reach the river bank and the sun again. It's boiling out in the sun. We've both got our bikinis on under our clothes.

We lay our towels down in the grass by the river and then lie down on them. Mary lies on her back and I lie facing the grass feeling the hot sun on the backs of my legs and watching an ant in the grass.

There is a big tree overhanging the river with a rope hanging from it. Mary gets up and I roll over and watch her climb the tree. She grabs the rope, swinging into the river with a big splash. She swims back and walks up to me dripping water onto me. I squeal and roll over.

I might go for a swim too, I say.

She climbs the tree again and I follow her onto the branch.

Bombs away, she says and drops in again.

I grab the rope as it comes back and wait for her to come up. She comes up and goes under again. I look down at her. Her head comes up again, but only as far as her eyes. She's being silly. I am about to drop in after her when I think maybe she's stuck. Her foot must be caught on something. I should get a stick. I jump down from the tree and run around looking for a stick. I can't find a stick. I can hear her splashing. There's one. There's one. Get it. I run back to the tree with the stick and climb onto the branch and lean over with it. The stick touches the water. She comes up gasping, and sees me. There! She's got it! She nearly pulls me into the water but I hold on with my other hand. She lets go. Her head is moving about, but it's below the water again. I hold the stick towards her and she is waving her arms about under the water trying to get free. She comes up and takes another breath and reaches for the stick again. I look at her and move it out of her reach so she can't get it. She goes down again and I sit on the branch holding the stick and watching the top of her head.

Now her head's stopped moving. She doesn't come up again. I sit there in the tree with the stick. I can hear the faint lapping of water. I am so scared I feel like I have been turned inside out. I get down and put on my shorts and top over my bikini and fold my towel up and turn round. The man is leaning against a tree in the shade watching. I scream and the dog barks as I run through the grass and get the bike and ride, ride, ride, ride as fast as I can back to the Smiloviches'. Please

God. Please God I promise to be good for the rest of my life.

There's no one home. The doors and windows are all wide open. I go upstairs and put the bikini back in the drawer, then downstairs and put the towel in with the last load of washing. I find the iron and the ironing board and go out the back and start taking the washing off the line, squinting my eyes as I look up, folding the washing neatly like my mother tells me to, folding stiff grey shorts and T-shirts and hankies, and when I've finished I pick up all the pegs that have dropped into the grass and go inside and start ironing. Mary's sister, Rachel, comes back.

Where's Mary? she asks.

Swimming, I say. I didn't go. I came home instead.

She says oh and gets an apple and goes outside. When the machine finishes the last load I take it outside and hang it up, then come inside and keep ironing. I like ironing Mary's father's shirts. I iron the collar and the cuffs first and then the back and the two fronts, ironing carefully between the buttons and then hanging them up on coat-hangers over the door. The Smiloviches have ironing spray. It smells wonderful and the iron glides over the shirts nicely.

I am sweating. It's hot even though it's now six o'clock. Mary's brother comes back. He looks at me funny. I remember the dancing and look away. The phone rings. Her brother answers it. It's Mrs Smilovich. Please God. He tells her that Rachel is home and Ruth, but Mary isn't. She went swimming. He says all right and puts the phone down.

Are they coming home? I ask.

Nope, he says. He goes upstairs.

I get the last load of washing off the line and fold it all up and put the towel at the bottom of the pile. A car comes up the driveway while I'm standing at the washing line. They're back!

They pull into the carport and I can't see them and then here they come. The men look at a motorbike in the carport and Mary's mother and my mother go into the kitchen.

Thank you, Ruth, Mary's mother says, looking at all the shirts hanging up. You didn't have to do that.

Very good, my mother says, raising an eyebrow. She's been drinking.

Has Mary come home? her mother asks.

No, I say and they start to get worried.

Kevin! Rachel! her mother calls, Come down here! Where's Mary?

We don't know, they say. She went swimming with Ruth.

I came back, I say quickly, I didn't go.

Well, where was she going? my mother asks me.

The pool, I say. No, that's right, the river.

The river? her mother says. What's she doing going to the river?

The fathers get in the car to drive to the river to bring her home. They're still talking about the motorbike. Mrs Smilovich says we're going to have fish and chips for tea. I want a spring roll. Please God. I promise to be good.

I offer to take the shirts upstairs but my mother says Go outside. So I go outside and sit on the hot lawn, looking at the clothes line and watching a sparrow on the carport roof. It drops down onto the grass and comes close enough so that I can see the holes in its beak. The phone rings. The sparrow flies back to the carport roof. I hear Mrs Smilovich yell out. Later the police want to talk to me but they just want to know what time it happened. One of the policemen writes my name down. My mother and father and I drive home late at night, down long country roads and I am supposed to be asleep in the back but I am awake and my sunburn hurts and I am watching the moon and power lines and clouds and listening to my mother saying, I can't believe it Alan. Only thirteen. What was the girl thinking of? And my father tut-tutting and me upside down in the back with the clouds and the power lines and the moon.

21: Forward and out

By the time that door opened every other door in the house was off its hinges. We never made it to dinner. Did we talk? I don't know. We communicated but I don't know whether it was verbal or not. Martin Myers became immaterial. Everything was open. There was no part of my brain, or the city, that remained closed, and no hiding place. Traffic lights were alien amusement arcades, great bursts of colour. I recall crouching in the corner of the graveyard talking to some flowers who were all wearing bonnets. Tracey was intent on climbing up a tree.

And yes, I remembered what happened to Mary Smilovich. I remembered who the man in the tracksuit was. And I remembered why I had forgotten it.

Was that Tracey screaming?

They found us in the early hours of the morning. Mace had come round on his motorbike when we hadn't turned up at the restaurant, and found the front door open and the place turned upside down, and called the police. They picked us up in the graveyard.

That was me screaming. Tracey was unconscious. She'd chewed the top of one of her fingers off.

Yellow jackets loomed and injected and reared away.

"Good morning."

A nurse. I was in hospital.

"How are you feeling?" she said curtly. "Not a particularly bright idea was it? We don't know what's going to happen to your friend yet."

Tracey was transferred to the psychiatric unit for assessment. She regained consciousness, but she was exhibiting signs of psychosis.

Faye was called. My story was: we dropped a trip for Tracey's birthday. One.

I went home from the hospital. I kept my voice low. Told everyone who called where she was. I stayed in my room. James avoided me. Tracey remained in the psychiatric unit for a week and was taken home by Faye.

I stayed away. Faye rang and I said I couldn't talk about it. I finally went to see Tracey six weeks later, and she was getting fat. Faye was feeding her icecream and chicken kievs, things for children. Her skin was red and blotchy, and her hair was lank. She was getting a double chin. They didn't know what was going to happen to her. Maybe she would climb back – it was a wait-and-see situation.

Faye was weird. As I watched her handing Tracey her food and cleaning up after her, it was as if she was winning for a change. Tracey looked resolutely into the distance, doing what she was told, saying things occasionally. She'd appear quite lucid for five minutes, and then she would suddenly stop and listen – as if she was on the phone. It upset her too – or our reactions to it did. She had a hushed conversation with Faye in the kitchen, and when they came back Faye said that Tracey would like me to go. I told them I'd send Tracey's things over. I said her finger didn't look too bad. That you couldn't tell.

I posted Martin Myers his jersey and he rang me. I didn't recognise his voice.

"How's Tracey?" he asked.

"Why don't you go and see for yourself. Did you enjoy your affair with her?"

"I wasn't having an affair with her –"

"Fuck off."

"I *fucking wasn't*. Nigel was."

"Oh, *fuck off*."

He fucking wasn't. Nigel was.

***

I packed up Tracey's belongings, but the truck driver missed a few things when he came to pick her stuff up. Some rubbish sacks of clothes and things. I didn't bother sending them on. I kept them and lost them, bit by bit.

I didn't visit Tracey again. I didn't want to know what had happened to her. I took up self-mutilation with a vengeance: a nightly treat before bed. I had full-scale panic attacks most days, and I was going to push the blade in properly, settle some old scores with myself, in the summer, when I saw Tracey's mother at the supermarket, and started writing this, and it seemed like there might be some chance for me, some hope of redemption.

This house has been sold and the new owners take possession tomorrow. I've said goodbye to Ray. It was no big deal, he's used to transience. I said I'd write. Maybe I will. I'm going to finish this now and then think about what to do with it later. I don't care who knows anymore. I've changed some of the names, and if anyone ever connects Tracey and me, then too bad. Come and get me.

I've been looking at travel brochures while I've been waiting for the taxi. I'm going to decide where to go when I get to the airport, which is quite exciting. I'm writing this standing at the kitchen bench, my bag is packed beside me, and the house is empty. The power is still on. I can make a cup of tea and finish up here.

That's a wrap everybody. Come on Nastassja, come on love, time to go home now.

I'm going to take my word processor with me, although I've just realised that I'll need to get a travel plug at the airport. I've left the little photo of Tracey on the kitchen window-sill. They'll wonder who it is.

Look, she's left this. Pretty girl, isn't she?

Not anymore.

Fuck it's weird how people end up.

I've decided I don't want to go to Utah or South Africa: I quite like the look of the brochure for *Waiheke Island, New Zealand. A sparkling jewel in Auckland's crown. Just 35 minutes by ferry from bustling, downtown Auckland, Waiheke Island is a haven for artists, known for its beautiful beaches and vineyards.* There's a picture of an outdoor cafe beneath a stinging blue sky *overlooking a spectacular view of the Hauraki Gulf.* Maybe I'll go there. I don't know. Get some sun. Lose some of this weight.

The cab's here. I've told him five minutes while I save this. He had no idea what I was talking about. *Save what?* he said. I laughed. Tracey's smiling at me from the window ledge. A big broad smile inside her miniature silver-plated frame. We're all laughing. It makes a change.

I think I know the way forward and out now. I've been reading the book on creative visualisation that I gave Tracey for her birthday. It was like it was waiting for me the whole time.

Books have saved me again.

I imagine Tracey clear and level-headed. I imagine Martin Myers making his first feature film.

Imagine yourself as a beautiful, free, happy human being and you will be one.

I like that.

More new fiction from DIVA Books:

Needle Point *Jenny Roberts*

"The bruising and the torn skin were worse than I had ever seen before – even the most hardened users protect their veins."

Cameron McGill is on a mission: to find out why her sister, who never touched drugs, was fished from a canal with needle marks all down her arm. Tearing through Amsterdam on her Harley-Davidson, Cam encounters radical squatters, evasive drug agencies and a particularly alluring policewoman. But it's hard to know who to trust in a quest that could claim her life as gruesomely as it took her sister's.

"Deserves to be read by more than a niche market... An excellently paced, well-plotted thriller." *Guardian*

"A fast-moving tale of revenge and retribution." *Time Out*

ISBN 1 873741 42 1

The Comedienne *VG Lee*

"There was nothing and no one left for me in Birmingham."

"I couldn't believe it at first – that Susan could switch from padded Valentines, eighteen inches high with 'Be mine forever', to not even stopping her car for me to cross on a zebra. If she hadn't recognised me with the added weight, she must have known it was my shopping trolley."

It's time for Joan to try her luck on the London comedy circuit. After all, everybody always said she was a funny woman…

"A touching evocation of loneliness and the complex relationship between an ageing mother and daughter. A light touch, a wonderful laconic style and spot-on humour made it a joy to read."
Andrea Levy

ISBN 1 873741 43 X

DIVA Books are available at £8.95 each from all good bookshops or by mail order on 020 8340 8644 (international: +44 20 8340 8644) quoting the following codes: *Needle Point* **DVB421,** *The Comedienne* **DVB43X,** *Emerald Budgies* **DVB448.**

For a year's subscription to DIVA magazine, call 020 8348 9967 (international: +44 20 8348 9967). UK £24, Europe £50, rest of world £60.